Write To Meow

2014

Edited By Lisa M. Wolfe

Grey Wolfe Publishing, LLC
PO Box 1088
Birmingham, Michigan 48009
www.GreyWolfePublishing.com

© 2014 Grey Wolfe Publishing, LLC
Published by Grey Wolfe Publishing, LLC
www.GreyWolfePublishing.com
All Rights Reserved

ISBN: 978-1-62828-069-2
Library of Congress Control Number: 2014955917

Grey Wolfe Publishing LLC
lú bóna na coróin

Write To Meow 2014

Edited by Lisa M. Wolfe

Dedication

We humbly dedicate this book to the cat; young ones, old ones, and all those in between suffering in shelters, waiting for their "furever" homes.

Perhaps through the writing contained in these pages, more humans will come understand the unconditional love and selfless devotion you bring to our lives, and open their hearts and homes to you.

No more homeless cats, this is our prayer for you today and always!

Acknowledgements

We would like to send out a special **Thank You** to all of the fine authors who submitted their work for this book. It is because of your dedication to cats as well as the writing craft that we have been able to produce such a spectacular tribute to our furry friends!

We also want to thank the good people of **Almost Home Animal Rescue League** who fight tirelessly day after day to make sure that cats find all the love, medical care, and comfort they deserve!

And finally, we want to thank **you**, the person who purchased this book and is about to read it. Because of your interest in cats, or perhaps because of the relationship you have with one of the authors, cats will be saved, cared for, and find a special place in loving homes!

Contents

Thank You, Authors!

We believe in the power of the pen. We believe that literacy is an important part of a successful life. We are committed to saving cats from death row, and we asked for your help. You responded with an enthusiasm we could have never predicted; and we are tremendously grateful!

The goal of this collection is to bring awareness to the plight of the thousands of cats that are currently suffering in shelters and needlessly walked into the gas chamber. 100% of the proceeds from the sale of the *2014 Write To Meow* anthology will support the work of **Almost Home Animal Rescue League**, a no-kill animal haven in Michigan, as they save cats from a fate that is death. Their important work is supported entirely through the generous hearts and hands of people like you.

This book is a collection of poetry, short fiction stories and personal essays about cats. The guidelines were simple: write something that includes a cat as a character, or a no-kill shelter as a locale. We were thrilled to receive such a diverse collection of words that will most certainly make a difference in the life of cats!

The purring voices of the cats you have helped, we hope, will be incentive for you to foster, adopt, donate or perhaps volunteer at a no-kill shelter in your area.

Thank you, again. Your words have made a tremendous difference in the lives of these precious souls!

1.

All Alone in the Moonlight
By A.J. Huffman

after *Memories*, artist Osnat Tzadok

A haunting tune resonates from antique
phonograph.   The cat is hypnotized,
as if knowing the notes were forged
in its image.   Tail twitching like a metronome,
it waits on the edge of the chair for crescendo
to fall back into silent abyss.   Whiskers
and window reflect the static that follows,
neither truly appreciating the absence as natural
form of applause.

2.
Aria
Mark Hudson

In the small town of McMillan Wisconsin,
a twelve-year-old girl is saving kittens.
With confidence she claims her mission,
and in history her role has been written.
She has gentle and patient persistence,
working with a pet shelter in cooperation.
Yet, she needs very little assistance,
she has got the town's adoration.
She works with stray cats by the dozens,
nursing sick cats back to a healthy state.
In her bedroom she gives them loving,
freeing them from fleas and from hate.
Without volunteers to foster these cats,
some would probably die without a home.
This twelve-year-old girl deserves a pat,
that is why she deserves her own poem!

3.
Ashley
Danny P. Barbare

Ashley under the bed, on her back
Down the sidewalk cat, my love
In the window waiting, pouncing
On our two pooches, Cisco the
Crazy Shih Tzu on top of her
Throwing his head left and right
Till Ashley is fed up gives him
A nip. Yip! Night time
Commando girl the house alive
Climbing the book case, in the
Pitch black, brought home another
Cat a no no.   She baptized my
Pillow and I had to throw it away.
She was my sweet heart, my little
Tabby, that rode under the seat of
The car everywhere I went, meow.

4.

Her Cat With The Butterscotch Paws
John Aylesworth

Her cat with the butterscotch paws
never left the apartment
except for shots and check-ups
and he died after fourteen years
without ever climbing a tree.
Sometimes he'd escape to the balcony,
stare at the splashes of green,
watch birds follow traffic patterns,
catch sight of a world full of butterflies.
She looks at these things now through a window
in a room with tubes and whistles,
no balcony, only shots and check-ups
in the room with a window
where she can see her apartment miles away.

5.

Cat Tales In The Glaring
Deborah Guzzi

Put purring sounds around me, yes, I'm the apple of your eye.
Your furry form is always warm, your purr is a lull-a-bye
Arms and legs entwine us, so strong, Mime and brother Sy
around a dreamy place we lay and picture summertime.
Me and Mama [Molly] cuddle with our wee Tom cat
like balls we bounce and then pounce 'till Mama tells us scat!
The glaring's full of mischief rivalry and combat,
Circle round see what we've found, it flies, why it's a gnat!
Round we go till dinner time, then back we go like that
The bosom warm, the cuddly form of our sweet Molly cat
Sun up, sun down, this is the life of Sy and Mime cat-lets.

6.
Cat Valentine
Andrea Dietrich

If I could be a cat, I wouldn't chase a mouse,
but if you put me out,
perhaps I'd choose to go and search about
for flowers I could snip with small white teeth
to carry home to you inside my mouth.
My mission then complete,
adoringly I'd greet you with a mew
and blooms strewn at your feet.
I think I might like that.

If I could be a cat, I wouldn't want to eat
kitty stews in cans or liver meat.
I think instead I'd use my feline eyes to plead-
entreating you to feed me from your plate,
and then when you had your fill,
perhaps you'd leave me ice cream
melted and unfinished from your bowl.
I wouldn't hesitate
to lick your fingers clean appreciatively.
Yes, I think I might like that.

If I could be a cat, I wouldn't want to sleep
alone and curled around some ball of yarn.
I'd leap onto your bed instead (I wouldn't make a peep)
and nestle in the cradle of your arm.
And if you reached to stroke my fur,
I'd place my paws upon your chest charmingly
and warmly start to purr.
If I could be a cat, I think I might like that.

7.
Cat Worship
Deborah Guzzi

Cats have always been with me
each in their own way
has run my house, has run my life,
and worried me when they strayed.

White cats like Alice's Snowdrop
or striped tigers like the Cheshire
Longhaired Coons from Maine
Now those really are a treasure!

Long whiskers speared the dust bunnies
underneath my rumpled bed's shell
and they found my missing sock
but they would never tell.

My Pixies paws smelled like popcorn!
Her tummy fur was sweet and long
I've heard folks have spun yarn from it
which kept them very warm.

I dream, of black cats I have loved
and tortoise shell "money cats"
I've thought of them as babies BUT
They didn't think much of that.

I'd rather have a cat with me
For the rest of the life I'm given
Oh please give me one more cat
before I leave for heaven.

8.
Catnap
Elisabeth Ward

Look at you
Dozing in the sun.

Hollows in welcome mat sisal
Soak heat from the dry
Redwood porch boards.

Air cured by altitude and
Sweetened by silence hangs limp
Reflections off frosted snow.

I think of ways to describe your comfort,
But they all come back to

The curled up cat
On the mat
In the sun.

Originally published in Naked Weimaraner: The Dogs, The Cats, The Rest,
Shaggy Dog Press, 2005.

9.
Cat's Charm
Alexandra Heep

Any ailurophile will gladly tell
Feline creatures rule and excel
Lissome bodies with opulent fur
Become cynosure for the debonaire.

Felicity embodied with chatoyant gaze
Regal poses full of epicurean grace
Capture even a pauper's whim
Chances of eluding cat's charm are slim.

10.
Cats Or Dogs?
Connie Marcum Wong

Dogs love to chase cats
And cats love to tease.
They race up a tree
Then do as they please.

Dogs love to play
To bark and sleep
But most of all
They love to eat.

Cats love to relax
On a warm sunny sill.
At night they chase mice
When it's quiet and still.

It's hard to choose
The best one for me,
Because I find both
Are great company.

I can take a dog for a walk
But a cat's right there,
Waiting to be loved
Curled up on a chair.

A dog gives you kisses,
A cat purrs when it's glad,
Both make you feel better
Whenever you're sad.

With a dog and a cat
There are tricks you can teach,
But which one should I choose?
I must have one of each!

11.
Catworld
John C. Mannone

Let us play with the catnip toys, while she videos us romping in the living room, the carpet—pilled under claws— already made soft. Cuddle skin-to-fur in her lap; the sweet mint breath is pleasing. It's a miracle of science: she is god, she is feline; we are mere humans.

12.
The Cheddar Gang
William Doreski

Cleaning an Augean stable
occupied by sixty cats
exhausts me. Drowsy, I slump

in the shelter's only armchair
and observe the sunlight crawling
across the asphalt-tiled floor.

A mutter of paws interrupts.
A mass of black cats moving
as one cat with many, many feet

scuttles across the floor toward
the bright south window. Cheddar,
a big shy orange cat, shuffles

in the center of the mob. Blunt
round face, he's a feral male
who timidly accepts extra food

and the most tentative petting.
I watch the cat-mass flow up cages
and settle on the window sill.

The clean room smells almost sweet.
Winter houseflies buzz and drop.
A lone calico paddles a toy

at my feet. A huge gray feral
putts a plastic ball from one
corner to another. Cheddar,

upholstered by his many friends,
frowns over his domain and purrs.
He may or may not remember

that last Sunday I cleaned this room,
and the Sunday before and before that.
His world doesn't overlap mine,

but we both admire the sunlight
as it filters out the winter cold
and silts a warm mesh on the floor.

13.
Chloe And Oscar
Melissa Grunow

I found her on the rug in front of the washing machine. The mid-morning light spilling in through the glass block windows cast shadows on the concrete floor. The floor was cold and she was cold, the rug not providing much warmth, especially in the basement on a winter day. The water bowl next to her had been left untouched. I set down her carrier, unclicked the latches and removed the top to place her inside. When I picked her up, she whimpered the cry of a day-old infant, her voice tiny and without energy. Her body was withered inside a space that she used to find confining, a space in which she would howl and hiss, a place where she peed all over herself when I first brought her home. She wasn't howling now. Instead, she stared at me, through me, her eyes dilated so much, they were black and hollow.

****

The first time I met Chloe, I was seated on tired pink carpeting in an unfamiliar bedroom on a warm May afternoon. The sunlight bent through the slats of the blinds and illuminated dust particles that hung in the air and on the worn, over-sized furniture around me. Aside from the few browning plants cascading down the sides of brightly colored pots, there wasn't any sign of life in this room.

Sandy sat down next to me. She looked composed for a woman whose mother had just died, far more composed than I expected. I hugged her when I first met her at the front door of the empty condo, but now I sat in her mother's bedroom and didn't know what to say.

"They're usually hiding under the bed." Sandy shook a plastic ball with a bell inside a few times and waited.

Tony emerged first. Mostly gray save for white on his face, neck, and feet, he peeked his head around the corner of the bedpost, took one look at us, and immediately lost interest. I had never had a boy cat before. Perhaps his indifferent demeanor was the reason.

My breath caught when the other cat crept out from under the bed. She looked young and agile. She strutted right up to me and pushed her nuzzling head into my palm. "Oh, aren't you sweet?" I said as I ran my hand over her unique coat.

"That's Teeny," Sandy said.

Teeny. The name didn't suit her. She may have been a runt as a kitten, but she was an average-sized cat now. It wasn't her size that was striking. It was her fur. She was red. A deep auburn with underlying black accents that weren't quite stripes, but weren't spots, either. I would find out later when I took her to the vet that her coat was called "tortoise shell." The bright auburn of her fur matched my red hair almost exactly. A fellow redhead; my spirit animal.

I instantly loved her.

These two had been alone for the past few months, having only each other for company. A family member would stop by every few days to give them food and water and to change out the litter boxes, but otherwise, the cats waited in a warm and dusty condo while their human, Sandy's mother, suffered a brain aneurysm, slipped into a coma, and finally slipped away. In the whirl of mourning and funeral planning and settling of affairs, the family had come to the point to determine what to do with the cats. Their preference was to keep them together, but how? No one could take both; most couldn't take one. Allergies, time commitments, financial concerns, space, were all limitations that prevented the two from being adopted together. A shelter wasn't an option either, as grown cats rarely get adopted, and certainly not together.

I had responded to Sandy's plea for someone to adopt them, and shortly after was when I found myself on that carpet with Teeny's paws on my thigh, lifting herself up onto my lap.

I turned to Sandy. "Okay," I said. "I'll take them."

Sandy helped me load food dishes, a litter box, and some house plants into my car. Since Teeny was the runner and Tony a little more subdued, Teeny went into the lone carrier, while Tony curled into a quiet ball on the floor of the backseat. Teeny, on the other hand, howled and hissed, and shook the carrier, desperate and angry. Then the scent of cat urine filled the car. Even rolling down the windows didn't help much, and I wondered if I had just made a decision I would regret.

I already had two cats at home who I was concerned about and a live-in boyfriend that I wasn't. I thought bringing home two new adult cats would be enough for him to finally quit the relationship and move out of my house. He hadn't worked in months, hadn't paid any bills, and spent his days watching television and eating the contents of the refrigerator. He didn't even know I was going to meet the cats; I thought for certain he would throw a fit when I brought them home. I was eager for his anger. I wanted to enforce the point that it was my house, and I would make whatever decisions I wanted concerning who I brought in—these two new cats—and who I kicked out—him three months later.

I knew that I couldn't call them Teeny and Tony without snickering each time I said their names. Pet names should have historical or literary significance; they should be names of purpose, regality, and legacy. Pets adopted together should also have names that complement one another.

Tony with his majestic, but aloof nature, Teeny with her rebellious outspokenness, I knew what I would call them within the first two miles of driving home with them in my backseat. My favorite novel, The Feast of Love by Charles Baxter, has two young characters named Oscar and Chloe who help to narrate the modernized retelling of A Midsummer Night's Dream. It shows how different people have direct and indirect impacts on our lives, how they change who we are, and how we share interconnected experiences as humans who seek love and acceptance.

These two had changed me from a thoughtful, frugal planner, into an impulsive, emotionally driven decision-maker. They had a kind of magic about them that I needed in my life and in my home in particular.

When I got home and carried Tony into the house, I handed him to my boyfriend and said, "This is Oscar," and before his surprise had a chance to register, I continued, "Hold him while I get Chloe out of the car."

****

Beige everywhere. Beige walls, floor, brown wooden benches. I rest the carrier on the floor, sit down, and wait. The tile has a dullness to it that could only come from incessant mopping, and yet the room smelled vaguely of fecal matter, decaying flesh, anal glands, all below the surface of a generic cleaning solvent.

I think of the germs burrowed into the dingy tile grout, then pick up the carrier and set it on the bench next to me. It's dark inside, and I look for her nose pressed up against the air vents, put it's not there. I poke my fingertips through the holes and reach until I can feel her fur. She doesn't respond to my touch.

Around us, a dog barks, scuttles toward another carrier, and is met with a hiss and a low growl. A collie comes sliding through the entryway and puts his front paws up onto the counter's ledge, panting, looking for a treat from the tech on the other side of the window. The crated animals cry and squirm, the leashed animals antagonize those in crates. In the corner, kittens on display for adoption chase each other, then curl up and nap within seconds.

I turn away from them. My concern is for the cat in the cage next to me. I never knew her as a kitten, but she is different from how I have known her as a cat.

****

Houdini. That was the nickname my mom gave to Chloe after the cat found her way into the basement ceiling for the fifth time. Even as I tried to block what I thought were her access points, I would come home from work to see her covered in cobwebs or find a ceiling tile out of place, or the light cover dusted with paw prints. After a while, and when I felt confident that she wouldn't get stuck, I gave up and let her explore. When I would watch television in the basement, I could hear here moving about the tiles above me as she took delicate steps around the frames and HVAC tunnels.

But the ceiling wasn't her favorite place. For a cat who didn't like to stay still, her favorite place was to lie on my desk next to my computer while I typed away. She'd stare at the birds out the window, watching, patiently, as they fluttered from feeder to feeder and eventually flew away.

Oscar had a perpetual look in his eyes as if he were annoyed with everyone and everything around him, except me. He would follow me from room to room, waiting for me to sit down so he could climb into my lap or curl into a ball at my feet. He never napped in cat bed, choosing instead the last place I had been sitting.

By then, the boyfriend had moved out, and it was just me and four cats. I was in my early thirties and had become the crazy cat lady my students teased me about. I didn't care. On Halloween, my friends met at my house before heading out to a party. Elyse dressed as a cat, and knelt on the kitchen floor, the cats gathering around her. It was Chloe, though, who attached herself to Elyse the most. They went nose to nose before nuzzling as if they had always known each other.

In the morning, Chloe dug deep into Elyse's overnight bag and snuck trophies out of the room: hair ties, barrettes, anything she could lug away without being seen.

****

In the exam room, a vet I had never met before didn't even let me finish talking, before he scooped her up and left the room, the door swinging behind him.

I thought I had heard him say, "She needs oxygen," but I couldn't be sure. She was just sick. If he would have listened to me, I could have told him. I could have said that she had been hiding under the stairs a lot, had been less affectionate with me, and had just started acting strange the night before when I came home from work before a date, and saw her lying at the bottom of the basement stairs, not greeting me at the door as usual. I could have told him that I had called his office right away and said she was sick and needed to see him, or someone, and his diligent office staff got me an appointment for the next morning. They didn't seem concerned, so I wasn't as concerned, because I knew once she had medicine or a shot or something, she would start to feel better, and soon enough would be crawling through the ceiling, antagonizing the other cats, knocking over my basil plants to make room for herself on the window sill, and pawing at the screen as the birds taunt from the backyard.

"She's gone."

I didn't know the doctor had come back into the room until he was standing in front of me.

I sat down slowly until the cushioned chair caught me. Gone.

I wanted to ask what happened, but I couldn't. I couldn't speak at all. The vet spoke for me. "She wasn't getting enough oxygen and was already showing signs of brain damage. Even if she had made it—"

He was leaving something out. He had to be. I went through the events again. The night before Chloe had been lying at the bottom of the stairs when I got home from work. I knelt down next to her, I pet her, I spoke to her in a soothing voice, but I knew she needed to see the vet. They were open for thirty more minutes, so I called. I spoke to a friendly woman who said to come in the next morning. I sat on the bottom step and waited. For what, I didn't know. My cell phone rang. Maybe it was the vet's office, maybe they had an opening. No, not them. I ignored the call. I ignored three more calls and two voice mails—"Where are you?" and "What are you doing?"—stroking my cat's cheek while the others checked in from time to time, their eyes on me before brushing against my leg and scurrying away.

The phone, ringing. Finally, I left. I went on a first date with a guy I didn't really like, where I had to drive us to a chain restaurant that he picked, a place where I nibbled on bad cheese sticks, while I tried to ignore his body odor and keep him from trying to hold my hand. When I got home, Chloe had moved to the rug in the laundry room. I covered her with a blanket, left a bowl of water next to her, and begged for morning to come sooner than it did.

"But she just got sick. Yesterday."

He picked up the file from the counter, a file that had a red sticker next to her name because last time I brought her for her check-up she fought the vet and the tech so much, that they had to wrap her in a towel to finish the exam.

Today, they had wrapped her in a towel again, this time to take her out of the room, and this time, they didn't bring her back.

"Cats are really good at hiding it when they're sick," he said. "Most of the time we can't tell until it's too late."

I stared at the floor until I couldn't see it through the tears. I hiccupped and sobbed, the exam table between us empty.

Oscar was the first to scope out the carrier when I got home. I opened the door so he could go in and see that Chloe was not there. He sniffed around it, and finally sat down on the tile, his dark eyes squinting at me.

After Chloe died, Oscar wasn't the same. He was stoic, and intensely affectionate, especially during weekends when I would lie in bed and watch movies, curling up on the remote as if he were in control of the television. The other two cats came around when they wanted to, but Oscar was my shadow until he died six months later. He declined quickly, like Chloe, but unlike Chloe, I don't give him a chance to suffer. I lean against the metal exam table while my regular vet shaves down a small patch of fur. I put a gentle hand on him, cupping his head. She dabs his leg with an alcohol pad, and prepares a syringe. I slide my hand down his body, his spine noticeably pronounced and bony in my palm. I watch his face. It doesn't change. He looks ready. His eyes close slowly.

Dr. Sims puts on the stethoscope and presses the chest piece against him. I meet her gaze, her apologetic gaze.

"He's gone," she says.

I don't sink into the chair this time. Instead, I gently remove his blue collar with the silver paw prints; clutch it in my fist, and nod, an empty carrier on the seat behind me.

14.
Cotton
Allen Kopp

There were five of us: me, a brother and three sisters. When we were old enough, we were taken away one after the other. I think my mother was a little glad to see us go. She was getting old and wanted only to lie in the sun and take uninterrupted naps.

As with all of us, a big one came to get me. He smelled funny, but he handled me gently as he put me into a carrier and closed the door. I cried a little and pulled at the door with my paws but I knew it wouldn't do any good—I wouldn't be let out again until I was in my new home.

The car ride made me sleepy and made me forget that I had to pee. I had ridden in a car before on a couple of different occasions and I knew how it either makes you want to throw up or go to sleep. I curled up in a tight ball, making myself as small as I could, and went to sleep.

The car went a long, long way from where we started but finally it came to a stop. When the big one got out, I stood up in anticipation of being let out. I was knocked off my feet again, though, when he picked up the carrier, carried it inside the house and set it down on the floor. A rough but short ride. Right away I smelled all kinds of awful smells that I couldn't identify. Was it the smell of another cat? My heart started to pound. All I wanted was to go back to the safety of my mother.

When the big one saw I didn't want to come out of the carrier, he stuck his big hairless, pink face through the door and spoke the terrifying language that to me sounded like a dog barking. I crouched down and backed up into the corner.

He upended the carrier—I tried holding on but there was nothing to hold to—and I went sliding out against my will. I stood up and took a few steps, stretched my muscles and licked my paw. The big one seemed to approve.

Just then a different big one, a "she" big one, came out of nowhere and scared me with her loud voice. I started to run for cover but she scooped me up in her paws. Now, I have to tell you it's an odd sensation to be picked up by something fifty times bigger than you are. I meowed a couple of times to let her know I didn't like what she was doing to me, but she nuzzled me and started scratching my neck and ears. In spite of the bad smells that made me want to gag, I began to purr a little.

The "he" big one said something to the "she" and they both made that hideous sound that I was to recognize later as laughter. They gave me some water out of a little red bowl and, after I took a good long drink, I was directed to the litter box, which I was very glad to see. I scratched in the box for a few seconds, sat on my haunches, made a tiny wet spot and covered it up so it didn't show.

The two big ones began playing with me, even though I was in no mood. They had a toy mouse on a string that they dangled in front of my face. I thought I smelled another cat on the toy mouse, but I obliged them anyway by batting at it with my paw and trying to catch it in my mouth. After they tired of this game, they gave me some food, which I was barely able to eat because it didn't smell like anything I had ever eaten before. I guess I was still too nervous to eat, anyway.

Later on they left me alone to do some exploring on my own. I went into the next room and then the room after that. I jumped up on a big table but there was nothing there that interested me so I jumped down. I walked the length of the couch and the chairs in the living room, exploring every inch of the stinky fabric; I stuck my paws in the dirt of some plants and then I climbed on the TV. I crawled under the couch and came out with dust stuck in my whiskers that caused me to sneeze. I jumped onto the counter in the kitchen, nosed into the sink and took a couple of licks out of a greasy skillet on the stove.

I went into the bedroom, which seemed to be the best room of all. The bed was soft with enough room for a hundred cats like me. As good as the top of the bed was, the underside was even better. It was dark and there were some boxes and things that offered complete concealment from any dangers that might still be lurking. I was thinking it would make a good place for a nap when Finley jumped out at me and scared me so bad I jumped sideways and took a few spider-like steps backwards. The fur ruffled up on my back and my tail puffed out to three times its normal size.

Finley was a young cat, not quite full grown, but bigger than me. He was a long-haired cat that made him seem bigger than he was and he had a mane like a lion. He let out a couple of guttural meows that to me sounded like war cries and came running toward me. I wouldn't let him get near me, though. I ran into the other room with him chasing me. I didn't know if he was going to kill me or just hurt me.

I dove under the couch and I knew right away it was a smart move because Finley wouldn't fit. He could see me, though, and he knew I wasn't going anywhere and that if I came out he would know it. Every now and then he stuck his paw under to try to grab at me, but I pulled away out of his reach.

I discovered then that Finley was the most patient cat in the world. He stood guard there, stalking me, for the rest of the day and most of the night. I was hungry and thirsty and I had to use the litter box, but I was still too scared to come out. When the big one tried to coax me out by shining a flashlight in my face, I just ignored him.

Finally, in the morning, with the big one there to keep Finley at bay, I came out. The big one picked me up and set me on the table in the kitchen to feed me. He spooned some food into a bowl and I began eating. When Finley, who knew everything that was going on, realized I was eating what he thought of as his food, he tried to get at me to push me away. The big one had to make him stay away from me so I could eat. (That's when I learned how to eat and growl threateningly at the same time.) After I ate, I had a good drink of water and a satisfying couple of minutes in the litter box, while the "she" big one held Finley in her arms and whispered in his ear.

After a couple of days I was feeling more courageous and I stood up to Finley, nose to nose. Instead of hurting me, as I thought he was going to do, he licked me on the face and head. I guess I discovered then that he wasn't as bad as I thought he was going to be. What I thought at first was meanness and aggression was more curiosity and playfulness, with just a little jealousy thrown in.

I was still leery of him for a week or so, keeping my distance and hiding from him if I found him a little too overbearing, but I began to get used to him after a while. If he wants the spot on the couch that I've made warm, he makes no qualms about trying to take it from me, but more often than not, I'm willing to move to another spot and let him have it.

Cold weather was coming on. Cats, as you probably know, are always looking for extra warmth. Finley makes a really good sleeping partner. Not only is he warm, but he has the softest fur I've ever felt. Sometimes we sleep head to head or cheek to cheek or crossed over each other like a couple of earthworms. Sometimes I use his belly for a pillow or he uses mine. When winter comes and the nights are really cold, the big one lets us sleep under the covers with him in the bed. There is no warmer place in the house.

Finley and I are now inseparable friends. We play together a lot and keep each other company. We're a lot alike but also a lot different. Sometimes we eat together out of the same bowl, but most of the time he lets me eat first before he eats. If anybody ever knocks on the door, I run and hide, but Finley stays right there to find out what is going on. When we both are taken to the doctor at the same time, I'm still scared but not as scared as I would be if Finley wasn't with me. When I hiss, he hisses, like two parts of the same hissing machine.

15.
Curbs And Chairs
Mark Hudson

While on vacation in Florida,
I went to a Mexican restaurant
with my sister. On the way out,
there were two stray cats waiting
outside by the curb. They looked
scared, confused, and hungry.

My sister and I felt bad for them.
But there was nothing we could do.

Then my sister told me a
story about her friend Lissy, who
put a chair on her porch, and a
cat began to sleep in it.

She had someone capture it
to see if it was domesticated, and
it was, so she decided to keep it,
and the cat was scared at first!

So she developed trust
with the cat, and now she
continues to enjoy fellowship
with her new cat.

16.
Dear Dying Cat
Andrea Dietrich

I saw your form, dear dying cat
On a winter's night un-snowing
Lying there across my path.
I rushed from my car unknowing
Of when you'd met with the fatal blow
That left you lying still.
Whether 'twas swift or painfully slow,
Your dying took not your will
For crouching beside you, I saw you respire
And chose to pick you up.
I desperately hoped you wouldn't expire
As your head I did gently cup.

I searched for one who would surely miss
Affections you must have shown,
And I felt somehow I'd be remiss
To let you die alone.
So door to door I nearly ran,
But no one gave a care.
Your eyes I frequently would scan
To see the light still there.
But then as I was cradling you,
You breathed your final breath.
I sensed your soul release. It flew,
And I was holding death.

Oh, could you tell, dear dying cat,
Before your soul did pass,
I cared? I quietly grieved, and with that,
I placed your corpse on the grass.

17.
Feline Friends
Deborah Guzzi

Fire, a most dreaded word,
FIRE—the shout, the smoke—the flames—
a nightmare where—heat rises and steam.
Where escape, escape seems hard fought.
Only life matters in such a scene;
only life would cause me to run
to hunt and search with all that I'm worth
for the most precious friend of mine.

I'd leave all the photos, my few gems and all
I'd search beneath couches behind doors
in the hall, until my breath left
and there was no air.
I'd search until I found my kitten there!
And happy I would be
if we came out safe
him and me.

18.
Forest And Moe
William Doreski

Forest eats alone atop
a towel-draped litter barrel.
Red patches decorate his pelt.
He looks drawn by Edward Gorey.
He looks harmless as a stuffed toy.
I feed Myra, Sassie, Jimmy
while he snorts his meal and purrs.

But when Moe, a white and black
and bulky neutered male receives
a dish of salmon, Forest moves,
dropping with a thud from his perch,
zooming close-up to snarl and push
and frighten away the other guy.
Moe cries and retreats, cringing.

Why pick on this timid fellow?
Moe hides under the bed. His face,
a black and white collage, clenches
with fear. How can we feed him
without arousing Forest's ire?
We thought he'd feel safe here,
upholstered by many other cats—

sixty of them, some larger
than Forest but none so fussy
about who gets fed in which order,
starting with him. Connie,

Missy, Cheddar, Gene, and other
favorites enjoy their little meals
with Forest smiling upon them.

Meanwhile Moe shudders and creeps
to a dish behind the sofa
where his enemy can't see him.
The room sighs a collective sigh
as cats settle to digest this week's
allotment of canned food, bellies
rounded, eyes glassy with sleep.

19.
Frosty, My Hero
Diane Gooding

Frosty, our fifteen- year-old Maine Coon, is my hero.

After Frosty had a minor medical procedure, she was blind and unable to walk. I learned some very valuable lessons during the weeks that followed her ordeal. She proved to be a very determined young lady. I am not going to lie and say it was an easy road for any of us.

She spent the first several days in a playpen to keep her safe. Either our friend, my husband or I stayed with her. We placed her food and water right under her nose and coaxed Frosty to eat. She forgot the concept of using a litter box. She cried for almost two days straight and hated her meds. We had to have the discussion that all pet owners dread; what to do if she did not get better.

Frosty surprised us by standing up one day, on very shaky legs. At that point, the playpen seemed to stress her out, so we put it away. We "baby-proofed" the living room with baby gates and removed items that could be dangerous to a visually-impaired cat. We helped her perform exercises to strengthen her legs and read countless articles on how to best help a blind cat. We watched her hug the walls as she circled the living room. She practiced walking; her little legs going in all directions and her feet coming down with a thud. She was quite the little fighter. When her back legs refused to follow her front legs, she turned around and hissed at them. We had to assist her jungle-cat efforts when she wanted to climb over some furniture, but we did so gladly. She practiced until she needed no assistance.

Frosty relied on others for a while to locate her food and water, but that slowly changed as well. We bought a water fountain and hoped that she would learn to follow the sound to locate it. We kept her food where it had been before her ordeal when we learned that blind animals rely on memory to locate most things. We returned her litter box to its former location. And it worked. The first time she found and used her litter box again, I admit I had tears rolling down my face.

Her walking continued to improve. We placed one of the baby gates at the bottom of the steps to keep Frosty safe, but she badly wanted over that thing. We had to physically remove her from the gate on several occasions. One day, upon waking from a nap, I opened my eyes to see her back end going up and over the gate before I could reach her. My husband and I laughed and rejoiced as we took it down permanently.

I really need to stop here and mention that I suffer from depression. Add in that my youngest brother passed away unexpectedly three years ago; and let's just say that I have been going through the motions and nothing more. But the day I saw Frosty go over that gate was the day my attitude changed. I found myself thinking about her ordeal and her determination and realized Frosty taught me a few things. When her back legs refused to follow her front legs, she turned around and hissed at them. So I have been hissing at my problems as well. When she was unable to locate her food and water, she needed to rely on others.

I have learned that it is okay to ask others for support. I do not have to travel this road alone. None of us do. But the biggest thing I learned is to NEVER STOP TRYING. Frosty drove that message home by surmounting her biggest obstacle, that baby gate.

Frosty, I am happy to report, has now regained her eyesight. She walks with a slight limp when she is tired. And she needs help getting on to her two favorite places, the bed and the couch. But that has not stopped her. She still has a lot of living left to do. And so do I. These days, we let very little get in our way.

20.
German Nightmares
Mark Hudson

My pen pal Marion had some nightmares,
and it's not surprising she had fears.
First, she dreamt of some type of being,
that appeared to her in her bad dream.
She is a teacher and she went to class,
and by her window a creature did pass.
She was kidnapped by the creature and
they flew through the window to another land.
They landed in a forest in the Middle Ages,
it was a dream that happened in stages.
In another dream there were noises she heard,
she could not see things or see a word.
They needed their English-German dictionaries,
suddenly something happened that was scary.
She opened the cupboard and a cat jumped out,
she woke up sweating and began to shout.
Needless to mention the cat was black,
my pen pal thought she was under attack.
Then she went to school and what did she see,
a black cat in front of school looking eerie.
She claims she's not superstitious, although,
the dream has made her a terrified frau!

21.
Gunner
Jen Camilleri

One of my favorite parts of volunteering at an animal shelter was the opportunity to take kittens home temporarily to foster as they regained their strength while having their food and water intake closely monitored. Many of these kittens were without a mom, or the runt of the litter and would need individualized TLC which could only be given in a home setting. I knew that with four cats and a dog of my own, I would be able to care for these kittens while giving them the opportunity to socialize with other animals. Lucky for me, my pets were very accommodating to these tiny little intruders and would enjoy showing them the ropes. I was able to experience the stress of waking up every three hours to bottle feed orphaned, newborn kittens. I was able to watch a tiny little runt of a kitten find her independence and eventually find her absolute dream home.   I have been fortunate to stay in touch with my of the adoptive parents and love seeing the pictures of my sweet fosters as they grow into loving cats.

I will never forget the day I was asked to bring a special kitten name Gunner home. Gunner was a cute little tabby who was having a hard time at the shelter. He wasn't eating very well or gaining weight as he should. I didn't really want to take another kitten in as I had just brought back a sweet little girl who was being adopted. I was still a little morose as I had grown rather attached to the kitten but it only took one look at Gunner to see that he needed some special care.

Gunner was very shy when I brought him home; he cowered in fear from the other cats yet seemed to find comfort in being near the dog. My two year old cat Truman was the one who always had a soft spot for the foster kittens and was the one who played with them and bathed them the most.   Truman was very concerned about this lethargic little kitten and paced before him for a while. We gave Gunner some subcutaneous fluids and eventually he perked up. He began to eat his food with gusto and used the litter box just like a big boy. Once he had his belly full, he morphed into super kitty. He began exploring the house and climbing up couches and curtains (much to my mother's dismay). He would climb on my mom and bat her glasses until she picked him up for a cuddle. He had a ferocious battle with a stuffed mouse before falling asleep in the middle of the floor. We tucked him into a special heated bed while he took an hour nap. After he woken up, he decided to make Truman his best friend. Truman played with him for a while, batting at him and playing hide and seek. However, when Truman tried to walk away for some quiet time, Gunner went with him.

Gunner walked under Truman's legs, weaving back and forth. They walked all through the house this way causing Truman to stumble a few times to avoid stepping on Gunner. I had never seen a kitten have so much fun. You could almost see him grinning as he ran with his baby steps to catch up with Truman. It warmed our hearts to see him perk up so much. We tucked him in for the night with a stuffed animal to keep him company and went to sleep. We never dreamed what the morning would bring.

I was woken up very early by my mom screaming that Gunner wasn't moving. I ran to his bed and saw him lying there, barely breathing. I wrapped him in a blanket and ran out of the house to drive him to an emergency vet down the road while my mom called ahead to let them know we were coming. I arrived at the vet after stopping twice to breathe air into his nose and begged them with tears streaming down my face to save him. The doctor took him from me and I sat down to wait. I was called into her office where she informed me that they gave him fluids and oxygen however he was not going to survive. He would either struggle to hang on for another few hours or I could agree to have his pain end.

After a few calls to the shelter, it was agreed that he didn't need to suffer. I was allowed to go back into the room to see him. What I saw was an absolutely angel of a kitten, with an oxygen mask on his wee face, wrapped in a heated blanket and an I.V. dripping into his leg. My heart broke as I saw his tiny little chest struggle to rise and then felt his body shudder afterwards. I nodded to the doctor and she took off his oxygen mask. I kissed his tiny face as my tears rained down on him. I whispered to him that he wouldn't be in pain anymore and he was going to a place with lots of animals to play with. I told him I loved him and that he had made me so happy in the short time I had him. The doctor met my eyes as she silently administered the drug. I continued to pet him and kiss him until he took his last breath.

I don't remember leaving or driving home. I know that the whole day my entire household (animals included) was mostly silent. We were all so sad thinking of sweet Gunner who never had a chance. All of us moped around the house avoiding cleaning Gunner's dishes or his bed. It wasn't until we noticed Truman curled up next to the stuffed animal in Gunner's room that my mom and I exchanged a grin as we thought of the fun Gunner had on his last night playing with the dog, the other cats, and especially Truman. I think we finally realized why he was brought into our lives. After all, he wasn't going to survive, yet his last night on earth he was able to truly experience life as a loved kitten. He was able to play to his heart's content, he was constantly being picked up and cuddled by us, he fell asleep under a warm hand, and was able to be sassy with some older cats. If I hadn't taken him home, he would have died all alone, with no one to comfort him in his final hour.

I had Gunner in my care for less than twenty-four hours, however never in my life has a foster kitten had such a profound impact on me. It helped solidify the importance of fostering and I was able to relay Gunner's story to convince others to foster. After all, if we don't open our hearts and homes to these helpless animals, who will?

22.
I Don't Like The Vet
Jennifer Koch

Written in the styling of "The Wheelbox" by Cate Caldwell (featured in Write to Woof 2014). Thank you for the inspiration.

The click and scuff of their shoes had gone past my cage a time or two already, but still; I was determined to get their attention. "Mew, mew!" I called at the height of my minute lungs.

I mimicked their pacing, refusing to give in. Back and forth. Finally, the miniature of the two stooped and clumsily opened the lock, "Look at this one Mommy!"

Mommy, the larger copy, leaned down and scratched my scalp, right between the ears. I purred. She smiled and called me a sweetheart, followed by a quick check to make sure she'd used the correct pronoun. I never understood why that was so important, but it didn't matter. They had picked me up, and I was ready to make the most of it.

"He's pretty!" the little one said after a few moments of giggling at my nudging of her face. Mommy corrected her and said that boys are handsome, not pretty. I didn't really care which I was, I just wanted a home.

"Have we made a decision?" asked one of the big people who took care of me in this austere place; they called it a 'rescue shelter'.

"What do you think sweetie?" asked Mommy.

"Can I have all of them?" the little one asked.

The bigger ones laughed, and Mommy dropped down to our level. "No sweetie, only one. How about this handsome fellow? He seems to really like you."

I purred louder and rubbed my head against the little one's cheek again to show her it was true. She giggled. "Okay, Mommy."

Was that right? Had she really picked me? Mommy stood up and followed the other big person a short ways away. The little one just sat and cuddled me. It'd been a long time since I'd been cuddled. All my brothers and sisters were already gone, and my own mommy had been gone even longer. I had started to feel pretty lonely, but now it seemed like I had a new family to play with. I didn't have to go back into the cage anymore.

After some talking and a few more head scratches from various others, they put me inside a strange box that I couldn't see through, except for the little holes high on the sides. I didn't like that box. It was dark, uncomfortable, and made me feel like I was moving faster than my little feet could go. I meowed loudly over and over again to get out and was greeted with an "it's okay" from Mommy and the little one, who I had learned was called Sarah.

I liked Sarah; she was doing her best to comfort me from outside the strange box. She even stuck her little fingers in through some of the holes in order to scratch me. I felt a little safer knowing she was still there. "Alright, we're home."

Home. That was the word Mommy had said, I was sure. I was home. Inside the strange, dark box, I tried to scratch at the holes to make them bigger. I wanted to get out and explore! I want to see it, my home. Feeling the box finally fall still again, the top popped open and Mommy reached down to bring me all the way up to her shoulder. The world seemed so big and vast from up here, and I couldn't take it all in fast enough. I wiggled around in her hands, mewing with excitement.

"He sure is happy about his new home," Mommy said, giggling as my tail tickled at her nose in my excitement.

"I want to hold him!" I heard Sarah call from somewhere down below, and I was handed off.

"What are you going to name him?" Mommy asked.

"Charlie!" Sarah yelled without hesitation.

"Charlie?" I thought, was I a 'Charlie'?

"Charlie?" Mommy asked. "That's what you named your old goldfish."

"I like Charlie," Sarah said.

"I like you too, Sarah," I mewed. She didn't understand me, people never do, but she scratched my head anyways.

Over the next few days, life was starting to turn into something I liked too. So much room to wander and play; I didn't much like the bell they put around my neck, but I managed to tug it off a feel times. Mommy didn't quite like that and kept putting it back on, but Sarah never seemed to care. And, me? I had a new home, I had a new family; I was happy. Then "that" word came up…

"Time to go to the vet," Mommy had said.

The vet. I didn't know what that meant, but they put me back into the strange, dark box, and I felt a bit scared. Were they taking me back to the shelter? It didn't sound like it, but still I worried. By the time the box finally opened up again, I wasn't sure what to think. The room I was in smelled funny, like dogs and other cats. I wrapped my tail around my legs and my ears dropped. Other animals always made me nervous, mostly because they were always bigger than me. Mommy scratched my head a bit, but I still wasn't sure I liked the room or the cold, hard table she'd placed me on.

After a few moments of timid exploring, another big person came into the room, and I ran back behind Mommy. "It's okay," she said and placed me back on the table.

"How're you doing little fellow?" the big man asked. He didn't wait for an answer, not that I was ready to give one, and started prodding me in lots of different places. My ears and my teeth and my backside, he looked at them all. It was a strange experience, one I did not like. Sarah sometimes tossed me around a little in play, but he seemed to be looking for something, like he was trying to find something wrong with me. There wasn't anything wrong though; at least, I didn't think so.

"Well, he seems healthy enough. We'll give him his shots and everything before we get going, but it looks like you don't have anything to worry about," the big man said to Mommy.

I looked at Mommy too, she was smiling, which I took to mean the big man was telling the truth, that there really wasn't anything wrong with me. I could have told him that, but people never seemed to really listen to me. I started hopping to be put back in the strange box. I wanted to go home. I saw Mommy pick it up, but she closed the top without me inside. I looked at her and mewed, she just scratched my head. "It's okay Charlie, they'll take good care of you," she said.

They'll take care of me? I didn't want them to take care of me. I wanted Sarah to take care of me. I wanted to go home. I mewed again. "Come on big fella," the big man said as he scooped me up and started scratching my back. "You'll see Mom soon."

"Bye sweetie," Mommy said and gave me one last scratch under the chin.

Bye... why bye? She thanked the big man and then turned to walk away, the strange box in her hand – me not in it. I was still in the arms of this stranger in this strange place, and she was leaving me. I meowed after her, but the big man turned in the other direction, and I suddenly found myself back inside a cage.

I clawed at the bars. Had I done something wrong? Had I been a bad friend? Why had Mommy abandoned me? After a few minutes of trying to escape, when I finally accepted that Mommy wasn't coming back, I curled up in one of the back corners of the tiny litter box they had placed inside with me. I fell asleep for a while, I'm not sure how long, but I heard the cage opening and blinked my little eyes in half-sleep. I felt a gentle hand pick me up, and I yawned as they pulled me from the cage. I started to stretch, but felt another hand grab me behind the head. I tried to turn around to see what was happening, but felt a sharp jab in my side and hissed in unhappy surprise.

I tried to jump down, to get away, but the hands held on to me. As I struggled, I felt myself falling back asleep and fought as hard as I could to stop it. But, I wasn't strong enough. Waking up some time later, unsure how long it had been, I felt groggy. I knew something had happened, and I knew something was terribly wrong. Something was missing. My tail's still there, so are my ears... no, it was my paws. My paws weren't right. My paws, the things I use to stand and play and jump and run... they were just stumps of pain now, wrapped in tight white and bloody bandages.

I wanted to yowl and cry and run away, but I couldn't even pick my small head up from the floor of the cage they had placed me back into. Everything was still a bit too blurry. Then, I began hearing the vague murmurings of a person coming to the cage, talking to someone else about needing to clean up all the blood and getting me some more water. Too weak to try and escape again, I just thought about how it was funny that I should need more since I didn't recall drinking any. I didn't remember much at all after Mommy had dropped me off at this place. She'd called it the vet. I don't like the vet.

I felt the person open the cage door and lift me up. Pain ran up my limbs; I couldn't help but bite them. It was the only defense I had left to tell them to stop. I didn't know what was coming next, but I knew I didn't want to find out. The person jerked their hand away quickly, almost dropping me, and then scolded me.

"That hurt," they said.

"You hurt me first," I wanted to respond.

They took me into a different room and laid me down on a blanket. I yowled the whole time as they remove the bandages. I tried to run away, but they held me. I tried to lick the wounds they had inflicted, but they held my head back, placing it inside some strange plastic ring. My eyes felt like they would seal shut from all the pain and hurt I was feeling. The people hurting me said I was doing well, that I was "such a good boy", as they wrapped my four paws back up in new white bandages. Each turn, the slightest pressure, felt like my paws were on fire, bone scratching against muscle. I tried to flex my claws, but to my shaky horror, my claws weren't there.

They had taken my claws. I looked up at them and imagined a life for them without the tips of their fingers and toes... yet they had taken mine from me.

Mommy came to pick me up the next day, cooing and cuddling me like I had done good. But, the only thing I could think of was, "What did I do wrong?"

I couldn't feel anything but pain and hurt, and I was scared. I thought Mommy was my friend. Did I really have to go home with her now? I wish I knew what I'd done wrong, so I could be sure not to do it again. I didn't want any more of me cut away.

****

Countless cats and kittens are needlessly tortured and mutilated every year due to public ignorance and the vet's bottom line. Declawing is equivalent to cutting off up to the first knuckle of your own fingers and toes and can leave a cat with lasting physical and psychological trauma. This leads to many being returned to shelters and quickly euthanized because they are falsely seen as "problem" cats. Help stop this by supporting The Paw Project and making declawing illegal!

23.
In Love With Another
Diane Gooding

I'm afraid I'm in love with another.
My husband does not seem to mind.
I admit I'm in love with another.
He is cute and very kind.
I confess I'm in love with another.
Deny it to no avail.
My heart, it belongs to another.
He has whiskers and a tail.

24.
Kitty: The Good Luck Cat
Sue Ann Whitston

Kitty, the half-Persian black cat with a white bib under her chin, looked confused. The woman who set the milk pan down on the porch this morning was beckoning with her hand to come inside the house. She held the screen door open as she cried, "Kitty! Come inside! There's a bad storm coming."

The cat bounced to the bare porch. Something was wrong. The folding chair was missing.   She adopted this family because she was treated with dignity.

The green eyes saw worry lines on the woman's face. A dark gray cloud formed in the west with a rumble.

Kitty did not need a second invitation. She streaked through the door and stretched between the pillows on the bedspread. She hissed at the woman until she felt the soft terry towel under her body which provided warmth and slept through the storm.

After the storm, Kitty returned to her patrol.

Kitty began each morning with breakfast after the Detroit Free Press delivery. She ate the clump of dry cat food – not liver, as her owner prepared chicken livers.

"Me-ilk?" which is Kitty talk for warm milk.

Milk was poured in a small pan with a bit of cream, heated to reduce the chill, poured into an old potpie tin, and set on the porch. She lapped the liquid, crawling on the folding chair for a bath and a nap.

As three members headed for school or work, she expected petting.

Kitty also enjoyed bits of grilled steak. She watched the man place an aluminum foil boat down on the driveway. She loved licking the salmon juice, and munching the bones and skin from the canned salmon, after which she groomed her long, black fur.

Cats with soft fur meant good grooming. Brush Kitty's head and under the chin, she would purr. Brush her back and sides, she would tolerate the brush for a finite period. She preferred licking herself. But without assistance from humans with scissors, the clump licked to a hind leg made walking difficult.

Kitty was an old lady by human standards, having raised four litters of kittens. Playful, she batted at sticks and the string attached to a plastic golf ball. Kitty was a good luck omen on Friday the Thirteenth. Crossing paths in the morning assured the family a good day.

While most cats use the litter box, Kitty would use the litter box in a dire emergency, preferring the outdoors. When she did use the box, she created mountains. During the winter months, she slept in a lined Styrofoam box in the garage.

Kitty was content to stay in that box all winter. The man would turn the electric heater on while she ate dinner and enjoy her petting. However, one Christmas Eve the windchill was a minus seventy-two degrees. Kitty was upgraded from the garage to the basement – litter box and all by two people who donned boots, coats, and scarves over mouths.

Kitty had the speed that was necessary for good hunters. She caught mice, sparrows, and a chipmunk. She patrolled five yards. Mice did not stay long in garages or yards with Kitty on guard. She liked hunting sparrows. One summer afternoon rainstorm, a pitiful "Meow!" issued from the front porch.

There was Kitty, drenched, with a dead sparrow on the mat. She was praised for hunting, dried with a towel, coaxed to the lawn chair, and left on the porch. Five minutes later, another pitiful "Meeeoooow!"

The cat was drenched again with another sparrow on the mat. After the third sparrow, the younger man watched through the peephole as Kitty crawled into low bushes in the neighbor's berm. The sparrows bathed and drank in the sidewalk puddle. He opened the door, unfurled the umbrella, ran across the lawn yelling as a banshee, and the sparrows flew.

Kitty glared at him.

The chipmunk was a different story. The older woman saw the chipmunk run along the cinder blocks at the back of the garden.

Returning from church, the younger man sat on the back porch steps, lecturing Kitty that chipmunks were good for the yard and helpful to gardens. Mice were not.

To Kitty, no animal should invade her territory. One fact that Tarzan, a short-haired black cat from across the street, would learn one summer afternoon.

The humans sat on the back porch.

Tarzan entered the yard and walked between the side of garage and the fence. Something jiggled the fence.

"Meow!" pierced the quiet.

Tarzan streaked from behind the garage. His feet bounced on the lawn and cleared the fence. Then Kitty appeared with a smirk.

Tarzan never ventured into the yard a second time.

25.
Knowing My Inner Cat
Elisabeth Ward

I was a cat in my first life.

My husband pointed this out to me soon after our marriage when he found me sitting in a tree. I thought everybody climbed maples. Wasn't that why they branched so close to the ground?

My husband was a dog person, getting to know me and my cat together. My cat, Reba, was probably a more interesting study. I had put in a bid for her before her mother's owner suspected her apartment-bound cat was in a family way. (I'd grown up in a suburb in the lull between the late 1940s' rising awareness of the benefits of spaying and neutering pets and the 1980s' growing insistence upon it, so learned early on how to recognize a pregnant cat— usually, but not always, one of ours—at first glance.)

"In two months can I have the black female?"

"That's my roommate's cat. She's not going to have any kittens."

Two months later the call came in.

"Do you still want the black female?" (Of course!) "How did you know there'd be one?"

From the time she entered my home, Reba's perspicacity astonished me as much as mine had astonished my friend. We were made for each other. Apparently, my two roommates soon learned, we were made only for each other. Reba was terrified of everyone but me. I'm not referring to shyness or a skittishness around strangers. I'm talking terror. She'd be under the bed until someone looked there and she'd zip out to hide behind a door, and then slip behind the refrigerator. There was no end of places Reba could hide. I tried to memorize them as she reappeared so I'd know where to look next time. When nobody else was home she'd meet me at the door after work. With others present, she'd sneak onto my bed in dead of night.

This went on for six years. During that time I moved halfway across the country and into a one-bedroom apartment of my own, much to Reba's relief. Although she had only one bed to hide under, the sound of me shuffling extra grocery bags alerted her to expect company. My friends knew I had a cat because I spoke about her—a lot—but they never saw her. Some of them humored me about the need to eventually outgrow imaginary friends. One good friend knew Reba existed because we'd taken a weekend trip to the country. That does not mean she'd seen the cat despite holding her during the drive, as Reba cowered on her lap, eyes squinched shut and covered by her almost prehensile tail.

One night this friend and a recent arrival in our office came over to gather around my fourteen-inch portable TV and watch a football game. Six years younger than I and twice my size, this new guy tripped over his feet trying to fit into my small apartment.

No sooner had he sat down than Reba low-crawled out from under the bed, pussy-footed across the tiny entry hall, jumped onto the couch, walked across his lap and settled down next to his leg. My friend's jaw dropped. I went and looked under the bed, half expecting to see Reba and wondering why she had silently allowed a neighborhood cat to come in through the open window. (She had been spayed the previous year to prevent just that from happening. Again.)

But Reba wasn't under the bed. She was on this guy's leg. And she stayed there. All evening. Through all the cheering, and all my shouts of agony when his Giants beat my Packers. She should have deserted him then. At least she didn't follow him out the door.

"Him?!" I said after he left. "You pick him? He's too young. I don't know him very well. He's just a friend and I'm keeping it that way. Besides, he's a Giants fan."

Two years later my husband, Reba and I moved into an apartment big enough for the children we planned to have. Because Reba was sure to be frightened of them we provided, among other places, a linen closet hideout. But Reba was losing her need to hide and my husband was learning the behavior of cats.

That was when he began to point out other idiosyncrasies of mine. They were nothing new to me, for I had always lived with a fondness for stalking birds and small animals, learning their habits and hiding spots. I'd stare at my tank of tropical fish for hours. I don't recall scratching anyone but I admit, not without some small embarrassment, to howling and hissing when angry.

I can put my paw, er, hand over my face, curl up and sleep anywhere. Although I love to swim, I really don't like to get wet. Being wet is a different matter, because there's only so wet you can get before you start to dry. A cat might not like to go out into the rain, but once there, if the hunting is good it will stay all night.

I hate perfume; seek high places for safety but fear coming back down. My home is my home. I might choose to share it with those I love, but it's best if they follow my rules. I need an order to my day, and if I live long enough just might spend twenty-two hours of that day sleeping or watching a tunnel in the grass. I hope I'll continue to avoid hairballs.

My husband also noticed this: When a blade of grass moves, I want to know why. If a large bird circles, I want to know what it's just spotted that I can't see. I often sense movement before our dogs hear it.

It was Reba who urged me to leave for the hospital when our second child was due. Our daughter had been born two months early so I didn't know exactly what to expect, except that he would not be born on his due date. Nobody was. Oh, the "he" was a guess since nobody knew in advance in those days—unless they had a catlike intuition.

On his due date I had awakened at first light feeling unsettled, and a little achy, and decided I'd feel better if I got up and took a walk around our apartment. On all fours. I don't recall recognizing I was crawling until Reba, walking alongside me, pushed at my thigh, my hip, my shoulder.

"But this isn't the way I'm supposed to feel," I told her. "And, I can't time my contractions with you poking at me."

Oh, I couldn't time my contractions? Here was a hint that should have been even stronger than Reba's. We dropped our daughter off with friends around the corner and arrived at the hospital fifty minutes before our son was born. Thank you, Reba. Again.

Thanks to my husband's quietude and patience, Reba had adjusted to having other people around before our daughter's birth, so felt safe outside the enclosure where we kenneled our baby every night. A newborn might be a sound machine, and a smell machine, but even when wound up it stays in one place. When our baby learned to crawl, Reba took to hiding by lying on the couch.

Who was more shocked the day our daughter crept to the couch and pulled herself up to stand? Higher ground for Reba offered both of them opportunity for quiet study of one another.

Only one of our teenage babysitters ever noticed Reba, who never left the children alone in a room with someone she considered a stranger, but would hide in the darkest corner, often under the drapery. "Do you have a cat?" She asked as we walked to the door. "I felt something watching me and saw eyes, over there, but nothing else. I was scared to go closer to look." Just as well, for I knew Reba's trick of closing her eyes to better blend into the background. A closer look would have precipitated a flying dash over the babysitter's head.

Reba was nine years old when our first child came along, twelve by the second. Was she mellowing, or simply accepting? Perhaps, I suggested to my husband during an introspective moment, Reba noticed that our children made me, a shy and socially reluctant adult, of necessity become more outgoing and interactive with people.

By the time we learned of her malignancy, Reba was fifteen and a regular visitor during our children's bedtime book and lullaby. The cat who never failed to tell me what I needed to know somehow failed to let on she was in pain. How could an animal who predicted arrivals—including her own—with such alacrity be so inept at warning of departures?

We all know the awful loss of a pet. It's not just the love, not that glorious all-encompassing pool of affection, the constant companionship, the little quirks. There's the reminder in that deep gorge of lost responsibility. My first thought every morning for fifteen years was to feed the cat. My last thoughts at night were Is she in? Is she safe? I knew where the children were because I put them to bed, and then Reba put me to bed. Although she'd awaken me with a problem, it was so I could solve that problem—ultimately for her well-being. For all the concern she showed me over the years, all her messages about my life, I had let her being well escape my notice. Not very catlike of me.

Yet, it is exceptionally catlike not to let on about suffering, to go on about business as though it's nobody else's business. I don't tell people I'm sick, and, if not contagious, do what I can to hide the fact. That notwithstanding, due to a feline's desire to sleep near someone warm and motionless Reba was no stranger to what I referred to as Ghoul Mode: rushing onto the bed of anyone feverish, supine and moaning. But for a cat that's a matter of comfort, not a matter of life and death.

The independence of cats and total dependence of dogs are well enough documented, but there's more to it than that. Cats take, or don't take, instinctively to someone. And that's that. Dogs can be won over. Horses, goats, even chickens, can learn to like someone, or to at least acclimate to them. Cats like you or don't like you. If they don't like you they can still tolerate you but there's not much point in trying to win them over. I understand that. It's not a question of fairness; it's a question of balance.

Dogs let you know they're alert to everything, and, unless they're up to no good, they keep nothing secret. But cats know it all first and only pass on the information if they think it's a) important to them, b) very important to you, c) going to cause trouble, d) a complete waste of everyone else's time. (No matter what the average person might think, cats never waste their own time.) How often have you watched a cat stare at something for so long you just have to get up to see what it is, only to see it is a Nothing? Cats love Nothings. To a cat all Nothings might turn out to be Somethings.

And, in those final days when a dog senses it can no longer protect the master, no longer amuse him by playing endless games of fetch, it will stay nearby for comfort. Sometimes, so will a cat. And sometimes a cat will choose to wander off to die alone.

Alone? I wonder if a cat is ever alone. What signals does it pick up? From where? And when it wanders off, who knows? It may be preparing for its next life.

26.
Lilly And The Tiger
By John Bayley

He was cold, and alone, and he was very hungry when he first heard the soft purring, and then saw her glowing green eyes looking back at him through the darkness. What was she? She'd been there for days just watching him, and for hours they'd just stared at one another. He was too small and too afraid to leave, and she was just too big to come inside the hiding place.

She brought him food and left it just inside the opening. He slowly moved forward, and he could see her just beyond the opening, watching him. The food was still warm, and soft, and once he'd eaten his tummy felt much better. When he woke he felt warmer, he noticed that she was now lying across the opening and blocking the cold wind. The smell of her fur, and the soft sound of her purring was so inviting that he went forward and lay next to her warm body, and soon he was asleep.

When he woke, she was cradling him in her soft tan fur; a protective paw holding him close. Gently and lovingly she cleaned his ears and then his face. He thought she was so beautiful; green eyes, tall pointed ears, and angular face.

When he woke again she was still there, standing protectively over him. He panicked when she began to walk away. He looked first to his hiding place, and then back to her. She stopped and their eyes met. When she purred, he ran to her without hesitation.

The sun was warm as he walked through the dew covered grass. Soon his feet, and his legs, and his belly were wet. When he stopped to roll in the grass, her commanding purr told him they would have time to play later.

They traveled for some time through the wet grass, and when he saw the person he slowed and then stopped. In his very short life he'd learned that persons were bad; they made loud noises, and they chased you. She seemed to trust this person so he followed her.

The person had white hair, and gentle eyes, and she was smiling at their approach. "Lilly, this must be the reason you didn't come home last night you bad girl. I was very worried about you."

So she is a Lilly, he thought happy to finally know what she was. Then he watched as she ran up and sat down, allowing the person to stroke her soft fur.

Then the person met his eye. Much like Lilly's, her eyes were soft, green, and caring. "We're going to name you Tiger, and today is your lucky day."

The person held out her paw, which was not covered in fur, and moved her long toes. Slowly he moved forward, and then allowed the person to touch him. Her paw was warm, and her touch was soft.

"Now that's a good little Tiger," she purred gently.

And that settled it. She was a Lilly, and he was a Tiger.

The person's hiding place was so much better than his. It was bigger, very warm, and there was food whenever you wanted it! He and Lilly played all day long, and then they would find a soft warm place in the sun and sleep. The person was very nice to them, and Tiger was very happy.

He woke in the morning and Lilly was gone. There was something strange about the hiding place today. The food was not in its usual spot, the cool fresh water was warm, and it was very quiet. When he found them, the person was still asleep, and Lilly lay close purring gently. He joined her and they stayed with the person for a long time.

Suddenly, there were loud noises and the sound of other people in the hiding place. When the noises got close, Lilly's purr told him to follow. Together they ran and hid as more and more people rushed in and out of the hiding place.

They made their way toward the opening and went outside. It had been a long time since he'd been outside and the cold felt strange. He followed Lilly across the grass, and they hid in the 'Pretty Flower Patch' and watched.

When the people were gone he and Lilly went back to the hiding place. It was now dark, getting cold, and he was very hungry. Together he and Lilly walked around the hiding place looking for the person. When they couldn't find her, Lilly led him to a special hiding spot where they curled up and fell asleep.

When he woke, Lilly was there and she'd brought him food. This won't be so bad he thought, and together they waited for the person.

The waiting went on for days. When he woke, the food was there, and Lilly was there, but something was wrong; she was hurt. She wasn't purring, and in the silence of their hiding place, she could only look at him, the glow had disappeared from her beautiful green eyes.

She'd taught him that when someone doesn't feel good, you clean them. So starting at the tips of her tan colored ears, he gently cleaned her. When he got close to her injury, she made a noise he'd never heard before. He moved the food closer to her, and then lay in front of the opening to block the cold wind from coming into the hiding place.

The next morning Lilly was asleep and the food was gone. He had never gotten the food before, but today he knew he must. He loved Lilly and she was depending on him.

The day was bright and cold. He took a last look at his Lilly and then cautiously left the hiding place. How does one get food? He wondered as he sat outside the person's hiding place.

"Tiger is that you?"

He turned to the little person he'd seen in the hiding place. Like the white haired person, the little person had always been very nice to him. He allowed her to come close and pet his fur with her paw. Her touch was warm and gentle.

"Where's Lilly? We've been so worried that you were both lost."

At the sound of Lilly's name, he turned and went to her. The little person followed him to the hiding place. Lilly didn't move when he stopped and groomed her.

"Lilly, Lilly are you alright?" The little person purred as she leaned into the hiding place. Then he heard a funny noise, almost like a sob. "Lilly you're hurt."

Suddenly the light was gone, and the opening to the hiding place was blocked. Together with his Lilly, Tiger sat in the silent darkness.

Then he heard footsteps, and the sound of persons just outside the hiding place. "Where are they Elinor?" The purr was one that he recognized.

"They're in here. I blocked the opening so they wouldn't get away. Lilly is hurt badly."

Light filled the hiding place and he saw the white haired person lean in. "Tiger where have you two been?" Then she looked at Lilly. "She's been attacked by something. We need to get her to the vet."

He watched the white haired person gently pick up Lilly and then they were gone. A moment later the little person leaned into the hiding place and wrapped her arms around him.

"She'll be okay Tiger. We need to get you home."

Home, that's what the white haired person called her hiding place.

The new hiding place was much the same as the old. It was warm, there was food whenever you wanted it, and there were warm places to sleep in the sun. Every time he woke, he expected Lilly to be there. He wandered through the hiding place calling out to her, and he never heard her soft purring in response. He wondered if like the white haired person, she'd just kept sleeping, and that made him very sad.

When he woke Lilly was there, she was grooming him, and her soft purring filled his ears. He fell back to sleep safe, warm, and happy.

29.
Litter Duty
William Doreski

Wood-pellet litter, thirty
or forty trays to empty
three or four times a week.
The smell permeates. I wash
so viciously my skin peels,

exposing starlight beyond.
A hundred and sixty grown cats
and a dozen kittens notice
how clean or filthy their boxes.
Trundling forty gallons of waste

per trip, I thread the narrow stairs
and pass through the huge garage
and punch an electric button
and lurch into the winter light.
Slippery trip to the dumpster.

Icy ruts score the parking lot,
and a mastiff bounds to place
his paws on my shoulder and lick
my face into submission.
He doesn't know the cats own me.

He doesn't know that this litter
with its impossible stinking weight
is likely to crush my heart.
The mastiff belongs next door,
where a clutch of youngish men

load trucks with wooden concrete forms
and prepare to pour foundations
on an industrial-sized plot
two states away. The dumpster
groans as I dump the litter.

Cats watch from upstairs windows.
Their perfect faces catch the sun
as they wonder why I bother,
why I don't just find a warm spot
on the floor and settle down.

28.
Margin Of Error
Matt Pearson

Moe stared out the window as he'd done for countless days before. Only there were no days, just a long and endless night. Always night. More than that, there was no grass to stalk through, no flying things or running things. No ground to stand on. Just night. That endless night came to terrify him, but the house was so small he couldn't help staring out into the dark for hours at a time.

Somehow he felt better when he was there by the window, staring out at the night sky that slowly arced by. It matched his sick feeling somehow, made it easier to keep the food down.

He'd always felt a little sick, a little dizzy. Like the floor was moving. He couldn't even jump in a straight line. He remembered vividly the time he somehow became stuck in the air. The room was moving past him. He screamed and tried to run, little feet frantically skittering for a foothold on nothing. Then he hit a wall and slid down it to the floor. After that, he stopped jumping. Except to get up on the little folding desk by the window where he stared at the night.

Then one day he noticed one of the lights in the sky becoming larger. He went about his life, eating and sleeping, sitting on his keeper's lap when she was there. She would stroke his neck and make soothing sounds that helped him relax. It was the only time he didn't feel a little sick. And each time he woke, he watched the point of light grow until it filled the sky.

And then the house shook and roared and burned. Moe, restrained and terrified, held firmly in his keeper's arms, hissed and drooled and was certain in his wordless way that he must break free and run away. Run somewhere.

And then it stopped. Things were quiet and the world felt different somehow.

She carried him outside. There was light and grass and trees. Familiar, yet somehow not.

His paws touched the ground. It wasn't like the dirt he remembered. Softer. A lighter color. An unfamiliar smell. It tasted strange. Something like the inside of the mice he used to eat before she found him, but mixed with the taste of the long black cables he knew he wasn't supposed to chew on. The tastes didn't go together very well.

He froze, his attention fixed on something. He watched it flit over the grass, bumbling through the air. A butterfly. Colorful, orange and black spots. As big as his head. Instinctively he lunged at it.

He hissed as he landed, having overshot the strange flying thing. He jumped again, and again. He didn't get stuck in the air anymore but something was still wrong. Now he jumped too high. Too far. He hated it at first, becoming angry and frustrated.

But there was a consistency to it. He could adjust. He jumped and jumped, leaping after the flying thing and missing by less and less each time as it bounced along through the air.

And then he caught it.

He pressed it with his paws, kneading it into the ground. He sniffed it. It seemed familiar, like the smaller ones he remembered. Before the little house in the night. He tasted it.

Ech. But chasing it had been fun.

He looked back at the little house, open and streaked with black soot as it sat there in the grass. Big sheets of fabric fluttered in the wind, orange and white and beckoning to be pounced on. The keeper was there with some of the others, bringing out boxes and taking them to the bigger houses nearby. Moe thought he'd investigate, but was suddenly distracted by something more interesting. Something else moving in the grass. He dropped low and stalked toward it. Slowly. Quietly. Ready to try his new extra-long leap on it.

I like it here, he thought in his wordless way as he moved silently through the grass, toward the next fluttering butterfly to pounce and the young trees beyond.

And so it was that after the Colonial Authority had declared terraforming adequate for full colonization and import restrictions on biologics were relaxed that Moe, whose name was short for Margin of Error after his chance rescue from an automated trash collector behind an office complex, became the first cat on Mars.

29.
Max, The Black Cat
Diane M. Gooding

There once was a black cat named Max.
In manners he was very lax.
He made children scream,
when on Halloween
he jumped out from under a fax.
He tugged at the sheets of a ghost.
He was not a very good host.
He made the clown cry,
and the witch yelled "Oh my!"
as he sharpened his claws on a post.
The candy he tossed to the floor.
And ran when they knocked on the door.
He did not want out,
but he did make them shout.
Especially the kids under four.
The kids left with all of their loot.
To scold Max the point was just moot.
Cuz he jumped in my lap,
took a ten minute nap,
and I told him "good thing you're so cute!"

30.
Menage A Trois
Deborah Guzzi

A possum fell in love with a 'coon
And they spooned by the light of the moon
In pet igloo they snoozed
cause the cat took a cruise,
they hoped he wouldn't come home too soon!

Well, Ole Blackie the cat was real fat
So, his pet food he shared "How 'bout that!"
all ate from his bowl
Or so I am told
By the jay in the trees bold chit chat.

Ah true love did we see in the three
the Jay thought why not let them all be
he stopped all the gossips
the biddy's and trollops
and encouraged this equality!

31.
Miss Kitty's Roamin' Holiday
Carol Hanson

Miss Kitty came from a large family. She wasn't exactly sure how many members were in her family, because every time she counted them she came up with different numbers. Her brother Delbert told her "Just think in multiples. That's how cat families arrive." Miss Kitty did notice that as her family got larger, more and more of her brothers and sisters would just go outside and roam about. Miss Kitty knew "Roam" to be a city, so she just figured that's where they lived, somewhere near that big Coliseum. She didn't like to roam about. She had heard on the extremely loud TV wall that it was a "big world out there."

Miss Kitty looked forward to food time. It wasn't much, at least compared to what the cats on the TV wall got. Sometimes a box was just strewn onto the floor, and if you were near that spot when it happened, you had a better chance of getting a smidgeon of food. The people didn't even leave us much to drink. I saw my sister Glenda drink from a mud puddle before. I guess that was better than nothing. It did look like that chocolate milk from the TV wall.

****

One day I was sitting on the dusty window ledge, when I heard a noise outside. It sounded like music, but without that dreaded thump, thump, thumping I'd heard coming from cars that always made my fur stand on end.   My brother Beau pushed open the screen door and out he went. In came a stream of flies. If there was anything more than cats in the house, it was flies. I saw

Beau standing near a group of kids, so I got my nerve up and I pushed the screen door open too. Shazam! It was different out here. I was a little nervous and looked for a litter box, a clean one if possible, but I didn't see one.

Beau was standing next to the wheeled box that was making the pretty noise. Aha! Now I knew! This was an ice cream truck. Hooray! I saw Beau at the end of the line, so I slunk on up next to him. Well it became clear really fast that we were not getting any ice cream. The best we could hope for was something to fall off the ice cream that might be tasty. Some things were hitting the ground so quickly, and then completely disappearing. "Sprinkles" Beau said, "Look for sprinkles". It was pretty sunny out, so I didn't know where we would be getting rain from. I got tired of this pretty quickly, so I decided to do some roaming myself. I knew as long as I could see the place where I lived, I wouldn't have to worry about being one of those "stray cats" people always talk about.

I meandered about three yards down, and there was a young girl sitting on a chair with her hands on her chin and her elbows on her knees. When she saw me, she asked if I was from "that" house. Despite the inflection in her voice, she did start to pet me. Whoa! This was groovy. Since I didn't know her name, to myself I called her Tabby. Tabby had a lemonade stand set up, and was just starting to get a couple of kids in her line, when here came the jingle jangle of that ice cream truck, and there went Tabby's business venture for the day. With that, she picked me up and held me on her lap stroking my fur gently. Nobody at my place ever did this, so I didn't know what to think.

Tabby's mom came outside and asked her "Who is your little friend Audrey? Is it one of 'those' cats from down the street?"

Tabby/Audrey replied that yes I was. Mom could see that the lemonade stand was going to be a no go for the day, so she asked Audrey if she wanted to bring the cat inside for a treat. I knew that treat was a good word from watching TV. Wow! The inside was cat free. No blaring TV, no bad smells, but again no litter box either! I wanted to make a good impression. The treat was milk, and it was nice and cold. Audrey asked her mom if I could stay for a while. I wasn't sure what Delbert, Glenda, and Beau would be thinking so I wasn't sure if it was a good idea.   But it was so darn cozy, I just decided to get into a ball and have some quality purring time. I knew for sure I had found the Coliseum!

When I woke up, I saw my three siblings on the front porch. I guess they were here to take me back to the place where we stayed. Audrey's mom said she wanted to make a home for us at their house. A home! Like Lassie has? Yowzers! My siblings were scurrying up now into the house. We were just rubbing back and forth in our excitement. Audrey's mom whose name I now knew to be Layla, was aware of the plight that my other siblings were living in back at the place where we came from.   Layla said it was going to be her and Audrey's mission this summer to find homes for each and every one of my siblings. I was so excited, I could have jumped through a hoop, but I was still working on that first impression thing.

Little by little, I saw progress that summer. Audrey had more lemonade sales and Layla brought out cookies to sell with them. They were going to raise money for "Purrfect Paws"—their new cause. I loved how that rhymed! More and more of my brothers and sisters were being taken away, but this time in loving arms. I knew it meant I wouldn't see them again, but that we were in a far better place than we had ever been in any of our cat dreams.

32.
My Cats Don't Care
Robert Hosner

My cats don't care that I take medication.
Rather that I lickspittle small diagrams
To their food dishes.   Also, they love the
Carpet paths I make for them thru
Incessant pacing.   What happens when
My cats go slack? They splay themselves onto
The cool linoleum that is slightly
Grimed, slightly pocked by the
Elasticity of eight years without replace.
In case you are wondering, there are
Two of them.   One is a lover of purrs,
Close shaven like a tuxedo, lean and plum.
The other has an attitude thicker
Than matted fur, hotter than any burning ash.
Ashes I call her.   Ashes of the animal shelter
That she set to fire by heat of body
And raise to lip. She hates lovers,
Wishes she could burn them all crispy
Then pile them into a soot.   So not
Sootness I call her.   So nots pull her tail –
She may bite. Look at her lickspittle –
It's foam and foaming round pursed lip.
It's a good thing she's small.

33.
My Lady
Andrea Dietrich

Dedicated to Callie Cat

My
little
calico
is a lady.
How delicately
she creeps along the bed!
As if to beg my pardon,
she apprehensively proceeds
until, finding the spot she prefers,
she settles, softly purring, on my head.

34.
My Lilah Vampira
Andrea Dietrich

a swap quatrain

She likes to nip; she likes to lick.
My foot might get a little prick.
I'll see it's her. That little pip!
She likes to lick. She likes to nip.

Attacking me with small cat teeth,
she comes at me from underneath.
She bites my toes so sneakily
with small cat teeth, attacking me!

In her small mind, it's just a game,
but I don't like it all the same!
To nip and run, my cat's inclined.
It's just a game in her small mind.

A paper scrap she'll start to shred.
And when I wish that she, instead,
would come and sit upon my lap,
she'll start to shred a paper scrap!

In moments sweet, she licks my hand.
Those times are fleeting and unplanned,
but for her mistress, they're a treat.
She licks my hand in moments sweet.

She gives a lick. She gives a nip;
I'd rather feel her small tongue's tip
upon my skin than one small snick.
She gives a nip; she gives a lick.

35.
Mystery Cats
Elisabeth Ward

They come from nowhere,
      a nowhere to us, anyway,
For we've not been there.

One evening, or one morning,
      they're here
And though they may not be ours
      we're theirs.

I've seen them, from horseback,
      miles and miles from anywhere
And followed their neat line of prints down
      fresh snow on country roads.

When does one decide it's time
      to first settle on a doorstep,
And then to settle on a lap?
      To go indoors, to accept us?

They're Mystery Cats,
      That's all we know.
That's all there is to say.

36.
Nicodemus
Danny P. Barbare

I like Nicodemus
I am a stranger
But he treats me like
  an old friend.
He gets me
As if he understands
He teaches me to be
  friendly;
When I feel like I'm
  getting a bad rap,
Like he
  a black cat;
By simply saying
  one word
So ever gently,
  Meow!

37.
No Bad Luck
Alexandra Heep

Shiny black cat
With golden eyes
Skinny or fat
She can surprise.

So do watch out
As in the dark
You cannot see
What does not bark.

She is stealth
On velvet paws
Good for one's health
She has no flaws.

To all, black cat
Should never be
thought of with bad,
erred zealotry.

38.
Old Tom
Andrea Dietrich

Eight times he looked death right in the eyes,
sometimes facing freezing nights when nobody heard his cries,
sometimes getting into fights with others of his kind,
left almost crippled twice, and one time nearly blind.
Another time he got run over by a car.
No matter, though, he had a mighty lucky star.
That old, bold, gray tomcat, forced to live outdoors,
often fell off walls but landed on all fours!
Now going on nine lives, Old Tom still thrives.

39.
Pizzicato
Elisabeth Ward

You still creep in,
　　　like Sandburg's fog
On little cat feet.

So does age creep up
　　　on you,
Filling out the body those
Little cat feet must
　　　carry, sucking
Moisture from your
　　　bones, slowing
Your pounce, stiffening
　　　your gait.

Gone are the runs,
　　　the trills,
　　　the glissandi
Of feline grace.

Now you step quickly,
As though glad to be rid of a note,
Done with each painful step
Your little cat feet must play.

Originally published in Naked Weimaraner: The Dogs, The Cats, The Rest,
Shaggy Dog Press, 2005.

40.
Power Cat
Beverly Offen

My cat believes my life and hers are one.
to see in giving I am being led.
Just who decides the rhythm of our day?
Whose home is this? Who lets the other in?
That captor cat I fear has final say;
she is my dearest friend, but alien.

to find if cats see color as we can.
The perplexed feline, after great distress,
saw red and blue—and puzzled about man.
It might be that the facts we're testing for
tell more of us than who's superior.

41.
Ranger's Fate
William Doreski

Ranger unhappy in his cage.
Little Ben thrusts a paw
inside, comforting the prisoner.
What has Ranger done? No one
can say; but when Gretchen's voice
ascends the stairs, Ranger cocks
his ears and growls. Little Ben
reassures him. I crack the door
and insert a dose of canned food.
Ranger scoops it up and grins
his pale orange neutered grin.

Later I clear the area,
unlock the cage and exhort
Ranger to roam and chase a ball.
Rumbling from corner to corner,
batting the ball and my dangling paw,
Ranger plays at being a cat.
As a kitten rescued from a wall
he seemed a normal smudge of orange.
Why is he now on Prozac? What grim
officious person did he bite?
Gretchen? Mary? No one recalls,
no one knows why we drug him.

Liberated, playful, he's all cat,
but one of the shelter managers
wants to kill him: unadoptable

and lacking a quality life.
That isn't going to happen.
Little Ben joins in the play
and the two rush around together,
their brisk little faces brimming
with the vital force Thoreau
treasured in everything alive.

42.
Rocky The Cat
Deborah Guzzi

Never having been without you, sweet catlings all, neither day nor night, cold nor warm can I remember without a purr. Cats, soft and warm, cats, curious and wild, cats most dear friends your almond eyes have always held mine. Years ago, when my son was just stepping into puberty, to combat the terror and the withdrawal of his affections; you most special of all dear cats came to me.

The papers scrawl left a trail to you within its cheaply curled paper pages. Shelter cats need homes, eight-week-old gray tiger kitten available. I could almost hear your mewl from a half hour south. The car with me in it drove quickly north to you, the tiny teardrop of you; best to get there quick before child or father had second thoughts. Plucked from a inner city roadside refuse pile, home you came with me, nameless and oddly quiet.

Within hours it was obvious you were ill. For a week, I fed you fingertip to raspy pink tongue. You struggled back from the brink. Rocky we called you, our wee little fighter! Can you hear the crowds roar? Nineteen years have passed since you came and first walked between the tulips of spring with the tulips taller than you.

Now, your claws no longer retract, your ears are a bit tattered from the fight of a country cat's life. The glorious long whiskers you had are gone, bitten, or fallen off. Bones hold up your unkempt coat. No matter how much I brush, baby brush in hand for you will not tolerate any "knot pulling." You no longer seem to purr with vigor or health, but then, neither do I. I know why you are here, dear Rocky the Cat and why you stay.

Our dear friend Tammy who cares for you in my infrequent absences told me why. She speaks to the animals like Dr. Doolittle. She asked you. "Why are you staying Rock? You're all skin and bones. You can go honey. Go if you need to." She said. With a look of pure disdain and an up turned tail off you when with the loud thought to her "Mommy still needs me I'm not going anywhere!" said the most loyal male who has been in my life for the past nineteen years.

43.
Rudy Ray Produkshunz
By Jon Moray

"I don't know how we're going to put this CD together without RudyRay," Kevin said to his wife Kathy, as they reluctantly began plotting their annual Christmas CD anthology that they would send to friends and loved ones. RudyRay, the adorable and musically inclined ginger tabby cat, lived a rhythmic, harmonious, fifteen years before the heavens took him as their own.

"RudyRay...I recall when your dearly departed mom, Lois, nicknamed him Rudolph the Freckled Nose Kitty."

"Mom and Aunt Marilyn really loved RudyRay. Do you remember when we discovered how he inspired each song selection?" asked Kathy, running her fingers through Kevin's long hair.

"Yes. We flipped a coin to decide between the Drifters or Bing Crosby's version of "White Christmas." The coin landed on the table 'heads' for Crosby until RudyRay pawed it off the table and onto the floor to 'tails' and confirmed the result with a melodic meow. Since then, our loving feline's decisions were made with a vibrating purr, as he lay nestled comfortably on my lap, while I stroked his reddish, tan fur," Kevin lamented, while recreating his petting motion in the air as if their departed pet was present.

"That was the beginning of RudyRay Produkshunz. Since then, our little critter produced annual themed Christmas CD's, and also created a Facebook page that he regularly blogged on. Pretty tech savvy for a creature without fingers," Kathy reminisced, with a warm crescent moon shaped smile.

"He is missed by many ears that enjoyed his seasonal compilations. I loved his creative themes. One year, Tropical. Another year, Rhythm and Blues. Still another year, devoted to cities and states around the United States. Now we must go at it ourselves. You and me, without a vibrating clue."

Kevin had written thirty-five potential Christmas song selections on a notepad that Kathy perused with pursed lips. The tunes list would have to be whittled down to about twenty to fit on a CD, depending on the length of each song. They volleyed several songs back and forth but couldn't come to any resolutions.

"'Zat you Santa Claus?...Buster Poindexter or Louis Armstrong's version?" asked Kevin, dispirited.

"Oh, I don't know. If only..." Kathy answered, resigned to helplessness.

"I know, I know," whispered Kevin, taking her hand in his.
Suddenly, a strong vibration emanated from Kevin's lap. He hastily reached for the phone from his jeans front pocket.

"Did you get a text?"

"No," Kevin answered, rubbing his chin.

"E-mail?"

"No."

"Breaking news alert?"

"That's just it. There is no reason why my phone should be vibrating," his expressions ranged from curiosity to puzzled.

Kathy squinted in deep thought. Her fingers tapped the kitchen table as she pondered what to say next.

"Poindexter," she asked, and paused a moment for a reaction as Kevin continued his gaze on his phone.

"Armstrong," she asked, almost in song. Kevin almost dropped the phone as it vibrated in his hand. His eyes shot up to meet hers amidst the eerie moment. They flashed each other a look that can best be described as a splash of fear, a dash of wonder, and a smidge of happiness.

This story was inspired by my cousins, Kathleen and Kevin, parents to the late RudyRay Wruck (9/19/98 - 3/23/14). Their love and enthusiasm for their cat brought wonderful melodies over many Christmas seasons. Like RudyRay on Facebook at RudyRay Produkshunz.

44.
Scooter
Danny P. Barbare

Scooter is a cat
Who likes to spat.

In spite
Of her bite,

I like to pat
Scooter the orange cat,

If only she'd learn not to spat
Like a good cat.

45.
Secrets
Mary Ann Back

I had a secret. I wasn't using my telescope to study the heavenly bodies of space. I was using it to study my new neighbor, Magda Gatto—the languid sway of her hips when she walked, the way her limbs surrendered to the salsa music wafting from her house, the shimmer of her long, black hair in the Arizona sun. I imagined her scent, and the sting of her long, red nails raking my back. Sheer ecstasy. Night and day I watched her, cataloging my observations. As a psychiatrist, my obsession intrigued me; as a neurotic, my illness diminished me. The line between the two blurred more each day, but the clinician in me insisted on analyzing her behavior.

Magda prowled the streets from dusk till dawn, returning home, hollow-eyed and gaunt—suggesting insomnia, promiscuity, or other self-destructive behaviors. Her frequent showering and grooming rituals, though tantalizing to watch, were clearly compulsive in nature. I wanted to believe her tiny quirks were charming eccentricities. But when Magda returned from her nightly escapades covered in blood that was clearly not her own, her symptomatology escalated to a new level. She was deeply disturbed with secrets of her own, and in need of help.

I invited her for drinks. My heart thundered when she arrived sheathed in black—a backless silk dress and fur shrug to guard against the chill of the evening desert air.

"Magda, I'm Tom Garfield. Please. Come in."

As I reached for her hand, I saw a rotting bird corpse cupped between her outstretched fingers; guts splayed across its yellow breast, neck dangling, eyeballs protruding like bloated caviar eggs.

"Jesus!" I said, taking the carcass from her. Strange; she seemed perfectly comfortable holding the thing, as if it were a bottle of wine. "Last week it was a rat, and the week before, two field mice. Freaking neighborhood cats. What's next?" I laughed, but a chill slithered up my spine as I discarded the remains.

"Someone's very fond of you, Mr. Garfield, leaving such tasty morsels on your doorstep."

Her almond-shaped eyes were breathtaking—bottomless green my telescope had never captured.

"Mrs. Garfield?" she asked, peering behind me.

"I'm afraid Gerri's stuck at work. She sends her apologies." That was a lie. Though she'd tried to hide it, I knew she'd taken a lover. Ours was a marriage of convenience. "And please, call me Tom.' I handed Magda a glass of Merlot.

"Your home is lovely," she said; eyes scanning, absorbing.

"Would you like the two-bit tour?"

We moved from room to room, eventually arriving at my study, where the telescope was mounted, her bedroom aligned in its crosshairs. How could I be so careless? Freud's theory that there are no accidents flickered through my brain. I bypassed the room, but she stopped, opened the door, and walked inside.

I needed a distraction. "It's nice to finally meet you, Magda. We should have done this weeks ago. People should get to know their neighbors, don't you think?"

"Absolutely Tom, though it seems you've had a head start." She chuckled, resting her hand on the telescope. "Don't worry. I won't tell." She nuzzled my jaw with her nose. "I knew you were watching," she whispered, then flicked her tongue into my ear. "Did you like what you saw?"

She rubbed her body against mine, offering long, wet kisses. We made love—the first of many nights. Her cries were uninhibited—feral; her nails drew blood from my back.

Even in my elation, I couldn't ignore the fractured psyche deep inside her. Each time we met, I tried to exorcise her demons. She was slow to trust me, but patience coaxed her secrets free.

"You'll think my dreams are madness," she said, locking her huge, emerald eyes into mine. "I'm standing in the woods, quivering and panting - waiting for the moon to crest in the sky. My cells begin to ebb and flow; collapsing and regenerating with every heartbeat, until I'm reborn as a beautiful, sleek cat. The scent of prey consumes me. Freedom calls and I follow. But at dawn, I awaken in human form and count the hours until night returns and I'm free again."

"Fascinating!" I said. "Is it a domesticated cat you become?"

She slapped my face. "There's nothing domesticated about me! Want to know the real me?" She hissed, nipped my ear hard, and then whispered what I had already known. "I'm the one who left those gifts for you."

She was acutely psychotic, but the closer we grew, the less it mattered. My desire for her was insatiable. The gouges she'd left in my back burned with infection. Fever ravaged me; the house confined me. I needed space and Magda at my side.

We lived for stolen moments, and the glorious evenings when Gerri was away. One such night, I waited for Magda to come to me. I paced the floor; my passion burned. The hour grew late. Gerri was due to return; yet, there was still no sign of Magda.

An unnerving thump came at my door. I threw it open. There lay Gerri; arms and legs splayed, throat severed, exposing the small, ivory vertebrae at the base of her neck; viscera protruded through a gaping gash in her belly. Behind her stood the love of my life in her truest form - a black and regal panther, tail swishing, and ears peaked, emerald eyes burning for me alone. She stepped forward, and washed in moonlight, straddled her magnificent gift, while licking me with her long, lover's tongue.

The proof of her passion needed to be scoured from my doorway, but I was already becoming, bones twisting and grinding—organs expanding and contracting. I would have to wash my hands of it in the early light of dawn. Finally, when no human trace of me remained, we raced the wind toward the call of the night—bound in blood, no secrets left between us.

46.
Simply Precious
Gay Pawlak

I don't think there could be a cuter little being on the planet than a Kitty Cat. I recall a Kitty Cat in my early youth that showed up in the trees outside our home for about a week or so. That Kitty Cat lived in the woods you see, and my parents never wanted us to play with it. They told us specifically to not go near the cat and to stay far away from that area. I realized later in life that the cat was actually a Bobcat, so I finally understood. To this day though, I believe that little Bobcat really wanted to play with us. Instead, we had stick to playing with our little domestic cat, Fluffy, and that suited us just fine. We could climb the trees with her but she always beat us back to the ground somehow, each and every time. We had her for a long time it seemed as a kid.

Anyway, years later my husband and I adopted a new family member, (no not a baby) a little Shih Tzu dog. Once winter hit, it was too cold to take her outside for a walk and play. She seemed like she needed a little friend to run and play with inside the house, so we went to the local pet store and adopted her a Kitty Cat. You notice I said—we adopted her a Kitty Cat, because she thought Kitty Cat was hers. They became fast and best friends for life. The coolest thing about the new Kitty Cat is, she had a bob tail. It was simply meant to be.

We had Kitty Cat for thirteen years and our first little Shih Tzu, Daisy for sixteen (I will have to tell the story of Daisy in the next book for dogs). Anyway, those two thought they were the same animal. They didn't know one was a dog and one was a cat. It's really unbelievable how happy they were. They played and slept together all their lives. They chased each other up and down the stairs, under the beds, under my feet, and lay in front of the fireplace on their backs together just warming their little behinds. You couldn't find two little beings more in love and happy. We made sure they were loved and cared for all their lives.

At about thirteen-years-old, Daisy, the dog, started to not hear or see so well, but Kitty Cat seemed like a youngster still. However, Kitty Cat sensed that Daisy couldn't do all she used to do. That was no problem though. Kitty Cat just hung out with Daisy, sat by her side while she slept and wherever I laid Daisy down, Kitty Cat would be right there watching over her. They would touch noses to verify they were with each other.

Then, I noticed Kitty Cat started going downhill. She had gotten leukemia and was losing weight suddenly. One day she was instantly taken from Daisy and us. I couldn't believe it. She seemed so full of life and this quickly took her. Nothing we did helped. So at the end of their lives, Kitty Cat was the first to cross Rainbow Bridge. I never thought she would go first, because Daisy had come from a puppy mill and had health and skin problems. She was at the vet a lot, so of course I thought she would go first.

Since Daisy was fourteen now and could no longer play and keep up with a cat, I thought it best to not get another until she crossed Rainbow Bridge. Fate stepped in one day. I stopped by the vet's office to pick up Daisy's special skin shampoo and a nine-month-old kitten was up for adoption. She was homeless and had come into my vet's backyard. Lucky for us, the vet was able to coax the cat into her lap, and knew she could find her a wonderful home. Well she did. I took her home with me and even though Daisy could not play with her, she would lay right by her side as if to say, "you are not alone now. I am here taking the place of your beloved Kitty Cat, so just relax and rest. You don't have to play with me; just allow me to lay by your side." Those two kept each other company until Daisy's passing over Rainbow Bridge two years later. (She's in the photo below. Her name is Misty).

Now Misty was alone, and kept looking for the dog. What did we do? We got her a Shih Tzu, named her Coco Dog and they think they belong to each other of course, not to us. They are now eight and ten years old and are tearing up the house with run and play (as you can see in the photo below, the chase is on but the dog never catches the cat), like the other pair, these two are thick as thieves. It is unbelievable how precious little cats are. They are the perfect little pet for anyone or any dog, if just given the chance.

Misty and Coco Dog took the places of Kitty Cat and Daisy Dog, whose lives live on in these two best friends. They have brought such joy to us and a smile each and every time we look at either of them.

~They are all Simply Precious ~

47.
A Set Of Strays
Matt Pearson

As you might expect from someone rummaging through a dumpster for some day-old fried chicken, Friday had his share of filth matted into his grey hair and a subtle hint of garbage stank that wafted about him. All of this he brought with him as he jumped, uninvited, into my old truck, plopped his grease-stained hindquarters on the passenger seat, and expectantly waited to be chauffeured to a more agreeable locale.

Friday became my companion from that day on. We were a matched set of strays, wandering through a world that didn't make a whole lot of sense, trying to avoid the countless dangers, hassles and irritations it offered up while snatching the best morsels of food as the opportunity arose.

And then big tentacle-monsters started falling from the sky, raining brimstone and twelve levels of suck. Kinda caught everyone off guard.

Eventually I got scooped up by the Army and taken to a refugee camp. I didn't want to go, but they didn't give me much of a choice. I didn't know what happened to Friday. My only friend was gone.

The camp was run by some reconstituted Fed entity. They were mostly good people that genuinely wanted to help, I suppose. It wasn't their fault they didn't have the resources to do much more than keep us uncomfortable. They managed to give us three meals a day, a place to sleep and the finest assembly-line medical care a post-apocalyptic failed state could provide to its surplus population, despite having us crammed in at near-double capacity.

Most of the others talked about a mythical "tomorrow." Tomorrow they'd be reunited with their families, tomorrow we would all be resettled to new cities on the coast, tomorrow somebody would come and things would get better. Tomorrow was crap. Always. Not even new crap.

I needed to get out.

I spent three weeks' worth of tomorrows going along, pretending to be "with the program" while looking for opportunities to escape. Every day was the same. Get up at oh-five-hundred. Stand in line for breakfast. I learned quickly that it was best to try to be in the middle of the line. The gruel started to get less runny about halfway through the big plastic shipping tub, giving it a semi-mush consistency that made it almost edible. So with a full bowl of semi-solid oat-muck in hand, I'd wander away from the others so I could suffer through my monotonous slop in relative peace.

It occurred to me that I didn't even know where I was. We'd been brought there in trucks, packed into dark enclosures and driven over crumbling roads. Then they herded us out into camp life. I stared out at the world during every meal, alone and wondering what was beyond my immediate line of sight. A fence, a concrete wall, some trees. That was as far as I could see. That was the entire world as near as I could tell, all that was left. Another small cage. Bloody depressing.

But one morning was all it took, one day that was different. I saw something moving out past the wall. I watched as it came closer, ruffling through the overgrown grass. Half the inmates saw it too and came surging over, hoping it was a big fat field rat or a possum that they could jab through the fence and somehow pull in for a bit of culinary variety.

I was ready to fight them, rip their skulls out the long way if I had to. No one was going to sink their rotten teeth into my friend.

We couldn't speak, at least not in words, but we understood. Through the fence and across the void of species and language we had an accord. Friday was going to get me out of there. How, we didn't know. But it was going to happen.

What followed were two days composed of long periods of intense boredom punctuated by brief moments of irritation. Anti-climactic, I know, but living in a fugee-cage and hoping for a cat to spring you is a recipe for uneventful days.

But that night we all got a brief respite from the tedium. Motion detectors triggered searchlights that jolted guards out of their daze and yanked on their attention. The inmates started to scurry over to see what the commotion was, causing an admirable disturbance in their own right. Predictably, this excitable mass of broken humanity made the staff nervous and kept their eyes off me.

The Land of Opportunity. I took mine to slip unseen to the only way out that wasn't a four-inch sewer pipe or a body bag.

I must have been curled up in that empty gruel tub for sixteen hours before a forklift loaded the whole pallet, stacked twelve deep, onto a truck. I rolled right out the front gate, then after a mile or so climbed out and tumbled off the back of the truck into the dirt. I was a sorry sight, I'm sure, covered in mud and stinking of rotting oats and sweat. But Friday seemed to recall that he didn't exactly cut a dashing figure when we first met.

He let out a loud "mrow" of recognition and rubbed against my leg, then he started purring louder than the old truck that was still puttering along in the distance. In that moment it didn't matter that we were in the middle of a ruined and utterly craptastic world with a shortage of foodstuffs and a surplus of giant sky-tentacles that grab folks without warning.

We had each other. We were going home.

48.
A Stretch And A Purr
Alexandra Heep

Green-eyed beauty up on the window sill
A portrait behind her of life, not still
Blue sky painted with shades of ivory
Autumn's breeze captures her feline fancy

Calico colors reflected in glass
Perched high above concrete, people, and grass
A comforting shape, she's contentedly
Steadied by a tail curved elegantly.

Slowly shifts after a stretch and a purr
Just to bring to me ... sunshine in her fur.

49.
The Cat Got Paddled
A.J. Huffman

she said, and I immediately thought, how lazy.
Feline or not, it could have at least grabbed an oar,
helped its owner row the craft, like that famous pussycat
who went to sea in an ugly-colored boat.   It's not
like a little work would kill it, and even if there was
some strange waving accident, the furry critter would still have
eight lives left.

"down the stairs by my father," she finished
her sentence, and I swallowed my previous
critique with total shame.   That poor cat.
I felt awful for it, and its ass.   Those wooden paddle games
are thin and cheaply made, easy for even children to break,
but I suspect repeated contact, even though fur would still hurt
like hell.   Not to mention the awkward discomfort that must
have ensued in order to get that retractable rubber
string affixed to its tail.

50.
The Cat Who Came For Christmas
G.C. Smith

February 17, 1962. Wedding Bells. Jerry and MiMi. Party time.

November 18, 1962. Nine months and fifteen hours after the wedding. Irish Catholic Mothers in a tizzy. First born is here. A boy. Big, feisty, squally.

May 13, 1964. Second child. A girl. Tiny, beautiful, serene.

November 15, 1966. We purchase our house and move into it in time for the Thanksgiving Holiday.

December 24, 1966. Jerry (with a different second name so as not to be a junior) is now four years old. Lisa is two and a half. We're snug in our new home and it's time to start a tradition.

We decide to tell the wee children that Santa Claus brings everything. The stockings that will hang from the mantle. The gifts. Even, no not even, especially the Christmas tree. And, Santa will not come until the children are snuggled in their nests. And the children must be sound asleep. Then Santa will come.

Oh yeah! That was genius!

Sending two hyper tykes off to sleep early on a Christmas eve is as easy as getting the same little ones to eat vegetables any other day. But, cookies and milk are left on the hearth for Santa at six-thirty and the babies are read to and tucked in by seven. Then the hourly check of the hyper little critters. Finally, around eleven, they're asleep. And, you know that they're going to be awake by five o'clock in the morning. I wish that we were as smart as they.

But there's six hours for MiMi's and Jerry's new tradition.

Idiots! Idiots! Idiots!

I'm sent to friend Bill's house to pick up the tree that he's storing for us. Then I put it into the stand, wrestle it indoors, and MiMi and I decorate it with strings of electric lights, delicate glass balls, shiny tinsel, and garland. We tack up the stockings and fill them with oranges and walnuts and candies and trinkets. We get the children's gifts from their hiding place, wrap them, and place them under the tree.

Ha, that's done. And, it's only a little after midnight.

Now the rest of the new tradition. I'm preparing lobster tails with drawn butter, pommes frites, and mixed greens. MiMi's gathering the snips and scraps left from the decorating and the wrapping of gifts. We eat the lobster tail repast and wash it down with cold Champagne. Not a bad new tradition. Not bad at all. And, it's just before two o'clock in the morning. We're going to get two or three hours sleep before hyper babies are up.

Our new home has an attached garage and it's there that we keep the trash cans. So, dishes cleaned, MiMi attempts to take the trash out to the garage. She tries the door from the kitchen and hits something that's blocking the door's opening. Quickly she pulls the door shut and snaps on the lock. "Someone's out there," she says. It is a particularly warm Christmas Eve and I have not shut the outside garage door. "I'll look," I say. "No," she says, "it could be a burglar, call the police." I'm reluctant, feel a fool, but I do so.

We wait.   Now it's going on to three o'clock in the morning. The police car, lights flashing, finally rolls into our driveway.   If there had been an intruder I'm sure he's long gone so I open the kitchen door to greet the policemen.   Something shoots between my legs, tears through the house, runs into our bedroom, and dives under the bed.   Me and MiMi and two cops in hot pursuit.

So here it is three o'clock Christmas morning and two cops and MiMi and myself are lying on the bedroom floor coaxing the biggest tomcat I ever saw out from under the bed.   Needless to say the kids are up.

We finally get the cat out from its hidey hole and usher the poor, frightened thing out the front door.   The cops have hot chocolate with us and cheer as the children rip into their gifts. Finally, sometime after four o'clock in the morning the cops leave but there is no way the hyper babes are going back to bed.   And there is a meowing at the front door.   I open it.   The cat walks in. We feed it.   It purrs.   MiMi and the kids name him Alexander.   A look at his size (he turned out to weigh more than twenty-one pounds) and I add "The Greater".   Fourteen years later the furry critter is still with us.

We loved that big old cat.

P.S.   Christmas tradition was revised.   From the next year forward the tree somehow, miraculously, appeared, fully decorated, a week or so before Christmas and gifts were wrapped before being hidden away.   But, the lobster tail and Champagne repast is still a tradition.   And we all remember The Cat Who Came For Christmas.

51.
The Cat With No Name
Tim Tobin

Thursday night came and Jim Tobias lugged twenty-five pounds of cat litter to the curb for Friday trash pick-up. Then he lugged a fresh twenty-five pounds from the car into the house where he dumped it into the freshly-lined litter box.

Jim sighed, happy that it wasn't the first of the month. That's when Marie changed the upstairs litter box too. He carried another twenty-five pounds down and then up the stairs. Jim decided years earlier that he could live without the cats, but his wife loved them.

If the cats went, she went. Marie made that point crystal clear to good ole Jim.

So he hauled the cat litter pretending it was just another chore to be done.

****

The cat-with-no- name touched the lives of the Tobias family more than any other.

Residents in their condominium development tended to be transient and people frequently abandoned their cats when they moved. One, bitter, cold day in January a skinny, grey cat with no collar appeared on the patio. Jim and Marie knew it was the sight of their three cats, Puff, Sam and Peanut, that attracted him.

Marie spent days just staring at the little critter through the patio blinds. Her heart broke to see him so cold and so alone. Jim was moved too. But he pointed out that their condo forbade cats and they already had three. If the Association made an issue of it, they would have to move or give up the cats.

And Jim knew which way that call would go.

For days, Marie watched the cat slowly starve and freeze in the twenty-degree weather. Finally moved to tears she opened the door and put out food and water. The little cat devoured the can of food and then rubbed against Marie's leg asking for more.

Marie desperately wanted to name the cat but again Jim pointed out that if they give him a name, he belonged to them.

Of course that's what Marie wanted.

The cold of January gave way to a blizzard in February but still the cat with no name came to the patio. Marie made a bed out of a cardboard box. She lined it with a blanket and put a few used toys in it. She placed the box on the patio and turned the opening away from the snow and wind. The small creature slept in the box.

One day Marie ventured onto the patio in boots and a coat with a blanket in her arms. She picked up the cat still with no name and held him to her warmth. The animal purred his thanks but he also coughed deeply.

Mr. Softy watched from the patio door.

"Oh, okay, Marie, you win. But he goes to the vet before he comes in. We have to protect the others."

Marie agreed and they took the cat to the vet where the doctor gave them awful news.

"A cancerous tumor in the throat causes the cough. A biopsy would confirm the diagnosis but even with expensive surgery, the prognosis is very dire."

So Jim and Marie paid to have the poor little cat put down. Marie held him close to her chest and Jim stood behind her and watched the light just go out of the beautiful yellow eyes.

The vet asked if they wanted to leave a name for the cat.

"No, No," Marie whispered. "He was just a cat with no name."

Mr. Softy wiped away his tear and shrugged his shoulders.

"Five hundred dollars and the cat was never even in our house," he muttered.

****

Jim and Marie Tobias grew old, of course. Along the way, five more cats kept them company until only Muffin was left.

Jim continued to muscle the litter to the curb every Thursday night. But now he carried two ten-pound bags. He took more steps but the strain on his heart was not as great.

Marie, naturally, would have had more cats but Jim finally prevailed.

"After all, Marie," he argued, "we don't want a cat to outlive us and force the kids to put him in a shelter."

Reluctantly Marie agreed. She grew old with her husband and Muffin who sat on her lap and purred. And now Jim had only one bag of litter to carry.

Every time he carried the litter out he swore he felt a cat rub against his pant leg. When he looked down nothing was ever there yet a faint meow drifted away on the spring breeze.

Marie left first to find her beloved cats. Jim was devastated, of course. Their small condo suddenly became as big as a cavern and just as lonely. Muffin kept him company although she only sat next to him. She never sat on his lap.

Jim knew Muffin was waiting for Marie.

****

The night Jim left to find Marie, their daughters and grandchildren were there to see him off. Jim's last thoughts were whether or not there was really a cat heaven. The family was astounded when his last sound was a chuckle.

"It'll be just my luck," he had been thinking.

****

Jim and Marie Tobias lie next to each other in Angel of Mercy cemetery. When they pay respects, family and visitors are certain they see the shadow of a cat evaporate into the brush. Others swear they see the tail of a cat disappearing around the headstone.

No one visits a cemetery at midnight. But if anyone ever did, they would see a shimmering grey cat with brilliant yellow eyes sitting on top of the Tobias headstone.

The cat with no name watches over the people who loved him, even if it was for only a day.

52.
The Cat's Pajamas
By Cate Caldwell

"If I can't find someone to take this cat, I'm going to have my brother shoot it," I heard someone say from the other end of the hallway.

It was a Friday afternoon at four-fifteen during the summer, which, at a university, means it was a little surprising that there were two other people in the building.   I was looking to make a hasty exit, myself, expecting there would be no one left to knock over on my way to the door.

But I like cats.   We had two at home, and, having just lost our dog, had room for a third pet.   While I suspected my colleague was not serious about shooting the poor creature, I also suspected that she might call animal control.   While that would be somewhat less messy, it was still likely to be a death sentence.

My head hit the desk.   Then I got up and walked down the hallway to find my colleague talking to the poor beleaguered administrative assistant.   She seemed as uncomfortable as I was with the idea of having minions do away with the cat.

"I would," she was saying, "but my daughter is allergic."

"So am I," my colleague said, "that's why I can't keep her."

"I'll take her," I said.   I knew I should consult my husband, but the way I found out about our second cat was through an email message that read, "Don't freak out. There's a cat on the screened in porch. I put him there. Going to the store to get cat food."

We named that one Friday, and he's still around. A Detroit alley cat that jumped in the passenger side of my husband's truck after work one day, he adopted Matt rather than vice-versa.

This new one was also apparently a Detroit alley cat which my colleague, Joan, tried to adopt before discovering that not only was she allergic, but the cat didn't get along with her dog.

I dragged Matt over to her house that evening. Joan gave us a copious supply of cat food, litter, and toys.

As we were walking out the door, she called after us, "One more thing."

We turned around. She hesitated as if deliberating, then finally blurted out, "there's a chance she might be preggers." Then she shut the door.

Matt and I exchanged glances and then looked at the cat. Tiny, she looked as though she could still be a kitten.

"I think she might be too young," I said, doubtfully. Matt shrugged noncommittally.

If there's one born every minute, then apparently that one is me.

Less than a week later, the Veterinary Technician held the cat's paw and made a tiny wave. "Hi, Grandma! Hi Grandpa!"

I face-palmed, and even groaned a little. We had room for a third pet, yes, but not as much a seventh.

Also, getting the cats acclimated to each other was proving to be more difficult than I had thought. Friday was having none of it. We had kept the new cat under quarantine in our spare room until we could determine whether she was free from feline leukemia and AIDS, but Friday could only peer at the door as if it were a portal to hell. Eyes wider than a tarsier, his ears lay flat against his head and his fur stood so straight he was almost round. If he had the power of speech, he would have been performing an exorcism.

We'd given the new cat the somewhat cumbersome name Hermione. Most of the people working in the veterinary clinic called her Harmony, other than the lone Harry Potter fan.

"Uh... so what do we do with the kittens?" I asked. "Will you take them?"

"Noooo," the vet tech said tentatively, "but we do have a list of animal shelters you can call."

Luckily, the first no-kill shelter I called said they could take the kittens, but not before they were seven weeks old. Thinking that I had dealt with that part, I went on to conduct some research on what went into this kitten voodoo. How long do cats gestate, anyway? How many in a litter? Would they come out with or without hair? Most importantly, was there something I was supposed to be doing?

The internet told me that Hermione would investigate the house until she found the spot where she wanted to deliver. Also, I didn't need to do anything, the cats pretty much had it figured out.

Still, I wanted to make sure she had a comfortable place, so I bought a fluffy cat bed. Our first cat, Zathras, took it over. Once he sat down, he defended that spot like Thermopylae.

So I tried putting down some older blankets, which went completely ignored. Well, Friday sniffed at them and then gave me the hairy eyeball. "Oh, you're choosy now," I retorted. "You roll around in dirt." Yes, I do talk to my cats.

Finally, I gave up and listened to the internet. We would find the kittens eventually. Our house wasn't that big.

On September 10, 2012, Hermione came downstairs looking a lot smaller. We went on a scavenger hunt. There were no kittens to be found in fluffy cat bed, nor the musty old blanket, nor the retired dog bed, nor the laundry.

Finally, in an upstairs closet which housed off-season clothes, extra kitchen utensils, and knick-knacks for which we had no room, we found them. Four of them, nestled in a box of old pots and pans and crumpled up newspaper.

They looked like squirmy little moles. Their eyes were closed up and their ears were so small that it was like they weren't there at all. They did have hair, though. Two were tabby and white like their mother, and two were white and black. Matt noticed that they were also all polydactyl, meaning they had more than five digits on each paw.

As we watched, one of them squirmed too close to the edge and fell into another box filled with excess mugs. She mewled. Hermione didn't appear to be in any danger of moving.

"Is it okay if I touch the kittens?" I asked Matt.

"I think so," he said.

"Does that mean that the mother cat will disown them?"

"No, that's a myth. It's not even true for birds," he said.

So I picked up the very tiny black and white cat and put her with her siblings.

Fearing that the kittens would get lost in the newspaper, packing peanuts and old silverware, we moved them out of the box one by one and onto a towel. Then we took everything out of the closet. We lined the floor with a sheet and then put the box back, this time empty other than a pillow.

"That has to be more comfortable," I said.

Meanwhile, Friday was still expressing his dissatisfaction. He was on strike. He refused to do his regular job of being cute and resorted to pacing the house yowling in protest. He also refused to share the litter box with the new family. He decided the bathroom rug was an appropriate loo under the circumstances and if I didn't like it, well, then I knew what I could do about it.

What I actually did was take all the rugs out of the bathroom and put a litter box in there. Friday's private toilet. He agreed that it was an appropriate compromise. We spent rather a lot of time chasing the other cats away from it, however, with only moderate success. As anyone who likes cats can tell you, you can't train them. You can only convince them that what you want them to do is what they were going to do anyway.

After a couple weeks, the kittens began looking more like cats. In order to tell them apart, we gave them temporary names, settling on England, Spain, Germany and France.   England and Spain were the tabby, and Germany and France the tuxedo cats.

Cats are curious, as anyone who likes cats can also tell you, and the only way to keep them from exploring is to physically prevent them from doing so (by, say, closing and locking a door). As the kittens grew, they became more and more adventurous. This presented a problem because our stairs are open and we could see no way of preventing them from trying to descend.

The first time a kitten fell through the stairs, we rushed over in a panic.   We carefully examined her, and then cuddled her until she squirmed to get free.   Then she just got up and walked away. We were relieved to find that even very young kittens can seemingly shrug off a fall from a great height.   We later referred to this as "The Fall of France."

By the time the fourth one fell through the stairs, we glanced over and said, "Oh, there goes England."

I began to understand my friends who were youngest children, and how they always got away with everything.

After several weeks of having the kittens, we began to grow attached to them, especially Germany.   She was easily the most intrepid of the four, and the most social.   She was the most likely to come down and join us in the evenings for tea and old movies.

Her markings were such that she actually had little white gloves and a black bow tie.   She was also a chatterbox.   All we heard was 'meow, meow, meow,' but I wondered what she was saying in cat.   "There's a bird outside, can't you hear it?   And a squirrel!   Do you think they like bitey games? Also, why are kitchen appliances so loud?"

She seemed to have a particular fascination with the hair dryer, as if trying to figure out how it worked. She could have been a little kitty Nikola Tesla, for all we knew.

"I'm worried about Hermione," said Matt. "I'm afraid that after the kittens go she'll just mope around the house looking for them and yowling. I've heard of cats doing that."

"Clearly we can't keep all of them," I said. "Maybe one?"

We agreed to keep Germany.

When week eight came, we brought down a pet carrier and cleaned it. I put a towel on the bottom even though I was going through towels like nobody's business.

After a scene reminiscent of an episode of Benny Hill, we managed to get England, Spain and France into the carrier. Feeling sad to see them go, we loaded them up into the car and headed off.

We pulled into the shelter parking lot as soon as they opened. I had printed off the email exchange from weeks ago which indicated that they could take them, which I handed to the haggard-looking employee behind the desk.

He looked at the email, then at the ceiling as if it had betrayed him. "Why, God? What is she trying to do to us?"

After a couple deep breaths, he looked back at me. "I'm sorry. This email is from the owner, so we will honor it. But we are overcrowded already. If you could keep them for even one more week, it would be a big help."

So we brought the kittens back home. Friday looked at us balefully. Zathras hurled himself at the cat bed as if daring anyone to challenge his claim on it. Hermione immediately began to purr and clean their ears. Matt and I looked at each other. I felt like a heel, but Friday had clearly put his paw down. Seven was too many.

A week later brought the same Benny Hill episode of getting the three kittens into the carrier. The same haggard employee worked the desk. This time, they took the kittens, though they were clearly not happy about it. They also took the towel. I hadn't been intending to part with it, but I couldn't bear to ask for it back. I also wrote them a check to try to cover expenses. He thanked me, but didn't seem cheered up at all.

Here is a shameless PSA for you: please support your local no-kill shelters by adopting animals from them. Also, donations never hurt.

While the European country names were cute as a set, the name 'Germany' was a little weird for a solo cat. We renamed her Pogo. She had a little jumping play-fight dance she'd do that reminded me of an old-style Pogo stick.

As soon as Pogo was old enough to be fixed, we made a vet appointment. You might think that this would be a straightforward endeavor, and you would usually be right.

My vet examined the cat, his face screwed up in confusion. "I can't tell if this cat is male or female," he said. After putting Pogo under anesthesia, he could still not tell.

"She might be a modified female, but her parts are not in the usual places," said the vet. "You'll need a board-certified surgeon to do this."

I found myself picturing a cult of hyper-intelligent, polydactyl, mutant Detroit alley cats who understood electricity and wanted to take over the world. She already had a tuxedo. All she needed was a monocle.

The surgeon confirmed that Pogo was female and performed the surgery, which she recovered from quickly. After Pogo and Hermione were both spayed, Friday stopped feeling the need for a private toilet. We incrementally moved the litter box room by room until it made its way upstairs with the rest.

Pogo and Friday are best friends now. She's still scrappy and starts a lot of play fights, which she usually doesn't win. Friday, the largest of the four, merely plops down and rolls over on her.

Though it was an unexpected journey, we are delighted to have all four of our cats. I wouldn't trade any of them for a lifetime supply of caramel macchiato. All the cuteness and joyfulness they bring is worth some hassle and occasionally cleaning up cat barf.

Our parents think that we are crazy cat people, that four is too many. I think that disappointing my parents is part of my life's mission.

One of my favorite things about cats is that they do not care whether you have a prestigious job or a fancy car or whether you look like a supermodel. They will totally size you up, anyway. And if they decide they like you, they like you for nothing but who you are. In that event, you have a friend for life.

That is, as it were, the cat's pajamas.

53.
The Great Migration
William Doreski

Pumpkin Corridor. A plastic
three-foot dollhouse hogs one end,
while cages mount to a big window
at the other. Shy cats huddle

in the dollhouse. Bold cats hog
the cage-tops and sun themselves.
Litter boxes sulk and fume.
Stainless water dishes shine.

With a rumble of padded paws
the shy cats erupt as one
from the dollhouse, thunder down
the corridor, mount the cages,

and topple the bold sunning cats.
The shy cats clutch the winter sun
and wave their paws in triumph.
The light rippling through their pelts

looks like a coating of chain mail.
The bold cats mill around, grumbling,
unsure of where to settle,
but refuse the vacant dollhouse.

For three days the shy cats remain
atop the cages. The fourth day
dawns with an organized rush
back down the corridor, back

to the dollhouse where they peer
with green and yellow glinting
at the astonished population.
For that day the cage-tops go unused.

On the fifth day the bold cats return,
without growls or grumblings, and lick
their paws as if they'd won back
their space through deadly struggle.

54.
The Legend Of Cyrano The Cat
David H. Kelton

Based on a true story

Cyrano rolled over and looked at his paw. It was normal-sized now, lacking the oversized-palm and the long tendrils humans call fingers. He looked around. He sighed as he noticed he was still in the cage. A second before he was dreaming and he determined to recollect it.

Somehow he had been a human being. But his pets were human too. Little humans, running around, struggling to use the litter, a litter that he had failed to clean. He shuddered and looked at his paw again, at how the dew claw was inconveniently tiny and high up on his arm. He frowned and pawed at it for a bit. How could that feel normal when just a second ago he was sure he had a thumb?

He wished he had never been given up. Try as he may he couldn't understand why he had. Nonetheless, he mused to himself, he was thankful for the shelter. He had food, a roof over his head, and the people there did their best to take care of him and the other cats, so many cats. But this place was strange, with close quarters, and he longed for a home with humans that he could call family. And his dreams, these crazy dreams. Why hadn't he helped his humans in his dream? Had he ever seen humans act that way? His mind raced over countless interactions, which got him thinking again of the countless tricks they taught him to perform.

The doors opened. "Show time!" another cat meowed to himself. Cyrano rolled his eyes and thought how this was definitely not show time. Show time is what he used to do, before his trainers gave him up. But, really, he knew very well what the other cat meant. Cyrano put on his best cute-face and stared intently at the visitors, doing his best to will them to adopt him. Many of the cats murmured to one another with expectation of who their visitors might be.

Today's visitors consisted of two adults and a child, a young little girl bent on getting herself at least one cat. "Mommy, Mommy, Mommy! I NEED A CAAAHHT!" she said with all the high-pitched glee that only an eight year-old-girl like herself could muster.

"I am aware," replied the girl's mother with a sigh. "You've only been going on about since—"

"Forever? I know! I want this one!" she squealed, her mouth going between bursts of babbling and smiling ear-to-ear. She raced to the next cage without bothering to breathe "and this one! Oh and this one too! Oh how cute! Look at the cute!" Cyrano purred to himself. He loved such exuberance. Humans always were cutest when they were little!

"Now dear, you're lucky I even promised you one cat! I still worry our dogs will make lunch out of the poor thing."

"Three cats?"

"One."

"Two!"

"One cat. Not three, not two. One. And if you can't decide on one we're getting none."

"Nooooooo!" She looked at her mom with the same giant moist eyes that Cyrano had looking at them.

And then nothing. The mother said no again and they walked out. Each cat gave a moan of disappointment in unison.

He stared at that door for a long while, hoping it would open to produce those humans again. But it didn't. After a time he resigned to close his eyes and dream again.

Cyrano didn't know how much time had passed when he opened his eyes. It was dark and mostly quiet. Except for an occasional creaking. He strained to hear it. There it was again. *My, is that irritating,* he thought. He looked around for the source. He couldn't see it. CREAK! Ah, it was far closer than he thought. It was his open cage door.

He stared at it like he had the other door. I should stay here, he thought. The people running the shelter were helping him. There would be more little kids coming through. Then, he thought how that was going. He put his paw out, almost daring not to touch the cage door. He pushed it open.

He squinted, waiting for the door to give another loud creak and for it to wake the other cats, or maybe even the humans. But nothing, just cool night air. He worked his way down from his cage to the floor. The cage metal reverberated a soft twang under the grasp of his claws. He looked around. Was he sure he wanted to do this? It made him a little dizzy. The world seemed to spin a bit.

And then, as from an unspoken reservoir, his training and agile mind kicked in. He trotted himself over to the main desk, and like it was no big deal, pulled the drawer open where he had seen the keys kept, pulled them out with his claw, waltzed over to the door, jumped up and jabbed the key in. He jumped up, turning the key and handle at the same time, opening the door. He left without a trace.

He had been wandering for a while now with only instinct to guide him. It finally started to hit him how alone he was. *No, I chose this. But why,* he thought? He happened upon a pear tree and curled up under it as the sun started to rise.

No sooner had he started to drift off than he heard helpers from the shelter calling for him. He wanted to go back. He wanted to go back so badly he was surprised his body wasn't being tugged along towards it as if by some magnetic force. *Do I really want to continue to count on humans making all the decisions for me? No,* he resolved, and with that darted off unseen.

He walked along a street. It wasn't busy but there was the occasional human. Who were they? Could he trust them? One yelled "Taxi!" and a cab pulled up beside him.   He zipped in before the door shut.

The man in the back seat told the one in the front where to drive. Cyrano sat motionless. A few raindrops turned into several and the taxi put the windshield wipers on. A good five minutes more of silence went by before the man's eyes managed to wander to the space only two feet next to him where Cyrano was sitting.

"Well hello, little kitty." said the man.   "No pets allowed in the Taxi, mister. I'm going to have to ask you to step out."

"It's not mine." said the man, opening the door to let Cyrano out. "Sorry kitty, I'd take you in but my wife says our little girl has her heart set on a cat from the shelter."

Cyrano paused and then forced himself out into the rain. Oh how he wished he did not understand English! *Stupid irony,* he thought. He sat flustered and soaked, watching the car drive off into the distance. It was a mission now. He started in the direction of the Taxi, following the muddy tracks.

The thunder crackled as if trying to break his spirit. But it just drove him forth. But soon the tracks met washboard and ended. He walked to the nearest house he could find, and crawled under the fence.

He looked up. There was a little house next to the main one. It looked as if it had been made for a cat. *I must be seeing things,* he thought. But between the rain and exhaustion, he walked right in regardless of the fact that it seemed unbelievable.

He didn't remember falling asleep but he must have. It was daylight. It was dry. The sun was shining. And there was barking. Lots and lots of barking. His mind raced. He should have been terrified.

"Mom, mom, the dogs found something in the old dog house."

"Oh my gosh!" said her mom, startled by the growling and snarling of her Rottweiler Roxie. And then it suddenly stopped. Roxie trotted up to great them.

"Mom, I don't remember Roxie being able to purr."

"Oh my GOSH!" her mom exclaimed again, noticing the legs sticking out of Roxie's mouth. Roxie bent down and spit out a very slobbered on Cyrano.

"Kitty! Are you okay?" they said.   The girl looked into Cyrano's eyes and gasped, "Do you recognize him?" "Oh my gosh, is that the cat from the shelter?"

Cyrano thanked Roxie for taking him to his family.

Over the years the girl and Cyrano grew very close; He entertained her with his tricks, opening doors and desk draws and filing papers in just the way that ordinary cats never do.   And she always took good care of him, making sure his litter was extra clean just the way he liked.   "I swear he thinks he's human" her mom would say.   And they donated and volunteered often at the shelter who still didn't believe the escaped cat had become this family's very special Cyrano.

55.
The Sister's Cat
Mark Hudson

A woman had a sister so sad,
her cat had died, and she felt so bad.
From this, the tears would not end,
for the cat was the sister's only friend.
The cat would sit at the sister's bed,
when it died, it brought the sister dread.
No human visitation ever occurred,
but the sister approved when the kitten purred.
She would stay by the bed at night,
a guardian angel with second sight.
Now, the cat is in another place,
and the sister has an empty space.
To be without a friend is not so good,
a pet can fill this need and it should.
But when a pet dies we feel such a loss,
no ball of yarn is here to toss.
So if you are a social butterfly,
enjoy it, because time is flying by.
There will come the day when you're alone,
where no one ever calls on the phone.
And you'll be sitting there admitting,
you wish that you could have a kitten.

56.
The United Furry Front
Gabrielle Gamache-Nettles

I guess I've always had a United Furry Front, though the name for my cats didn't come about until I became a widow.

I've had cats pretty much my entire life. They all meant the world to me, especially when the outside chaos would come roaring through my life, upending everything, especially my sanity, in its path.

Whenever I made bad decisions, or I've had those rough days, or I was inconsolable, those hairball-emitting, purring and incessantly spoiled, whiskered animals would curl up in my lap, loving all of my pain away.

Because of this, I've always seen my cats as adoring cuddle companions. They meowed, chased after laser lights, slept in the most insane yoga-like positions, and if you were lucky, moused and kept vermin at bay.

Cuddle companions, yes. Soldiers, no. How could I ever equate these cosseted cats to furry freedom fighters? Well, maybe they didn't strap on an AR-15 with a band of bullets and meow "Viva La Revolution" to other cats, but they proved themselves more loyal than many humans I've known.

The cats serve as a front against loneliness, a barrier against grief, and a wall of love.

They push their heads against your body to remind you that you are loved, are worthy of companionship and are needed to give them comfort.

They play with lasers and toilet paper to make you laugh. They bat balls of crumpled paper to make you see that life is too serious and to just kick back and push stuff around, just for the heck of it.

They jump up and meow when you get home, and there are times where you wonder how you ever got along without them. You look forward to getting home from work each day. You love petting them, hearing their soft purring, that little engine of comfort, churning for you. They are there for you, furry, soft and sound. The United Furry Front. The stalwart, cute, hairy guardians of love.

With that said, let me introduce to you my own United Furry Front.

TOM

My cat, Tom, was legendary. Like all of my other cats, though, he had humble beginnings. I was seven years old, and I had lost my dad that summer to stomach cancer.

My mom saw how lonely and devastated I was, and decided to adopt a cat and a dog from the local pound. This kitty was Tom's mom. She was a beautiful black cat that we found out was pregnant, mere weeks after we got her home. (She went from being named Tom to Thomasina pretty quickly). Sadly, Thomasina ran away after she gave birth to three kittens.

We found homes for all of her babies, even Tom, the rascally black and white tuxedo marked kitten that dominated the litter.

Our cousins took him in, but as we found out, Tom didn't quite get along with their sleek, elegant, female Siamese that roamed and ruled their expansive home.

So Tom came back to live with us in our modest but comfortable house. I was overjoyed, because I missed Thomasina and longed for a cat companion for Rosa, our pretty curly-haired white dog.

Our cousin's Siamese was elegant, but Tom stood out as a dapper, regal cat with his own bearings. He had become used to the finer life with our cousins, and so walked with imperative authority around our house. He had unusual, scroll-like white markings that divided his silky black coat in half down his back, and he had a black mask over a white face and deep pink nose. My mom, ever the snarky one when it came to cats, called him "Cary Grant." I called him mine.

The years following my father's death were very rough on my mom and me. We survived, but it wore on us. My mom would make meals last throughout the weeks, and of course, I became what was known back then as a "latchkey" kid, pulling her homemade stuff out of the freezer to warm up each evening before she came home from work.

Although I was alone, Tom was there, purring up to me, leaping in my lap, and always, always comforting me. Despite all of my fears, anger and overwhelming confusion following my dad's untimely passing, Tom's presence kept me going.

He didn't know how crucial he was to my survival, but I sure know now.

Tom, though, proved that no matter how well we might dress, our true nature always reveals itself. Tom was an inside, outside cat (it was the 1970s, before I knew any better. Don't judge me.)

We soon found out what Tom was like underneath that unruffled, smooth coat of his. This was a cat that had a lot to prove to the other furballs in our neighborhood. He had bigger obstacles than his pedigreed looks, though: our cousins had declawed him after they had him neutered.

But like other cats who have been declawed and who still rub their soft paws on furniture, it's as if those little Ginsu knives never left their body. For Tom, it was a mere bump in the road. Cary Grant would prove himself to be more like Grizzly Adams in a tuxedo, or James Bond (if 007 were ever a great white hunter). Normal presents from Tom included massive rats, cute little rabbits, big, fluffy birds and countless mice. He had the most voracious appetite for outside animals than any other cat I've known. I remember my mom opening the front door to get the paper and screaming at the top of her lungs. I ran up behind her to see what the matter was, only to find a huge, headless rat placed in the center of the doormat, looking like some grisly prop for a horror movie or ancient curse.

"That thing is bigger than Tom! For a cockless cat, he's sure got some balls!" she said. Tom was quite brazen, too. Stealth was not part of his hunting package. He'd meow as he was approaching whatever animal he preyed on.

One evening, as I was getting ready for bed, Tom came skulking into my room, meowing funnily. I crouched down to pet him, and out popped a cute, tiny mouse. Before I could do anything to save it, Tom glared at me and engulfed his adorable hors d'oeuvre in one bite.

Like any other successful man, though, Tom the cat had enemies, too.

There was a massive grey alley cat that often fought with Tom. This is where Tom's mettle, and mine, was tested. Tom was roughed up so badly that he went missing for a couple of days. I started crying, but my mom told me not to look for him. "He's probably dead, honey. You won't find him." I was shocked at what she said, but even more so, I was determined to find him, dead or not.

I walked around my neighborhood, calling his name. Nothing. I went seven blocks away (I was about ten at the time, so you have to see this as travelling to the edge of the world for me). As desperation began to take hold, though, and I thought I'd lost my beautiful, handsome cat forever, inspiration broke through. A beacon of hope was seen in the few slices of Italian bologna my mom had in the fridge. I dug them out, the garlic-laden slices of processed meat, and began to wave them around as I trekked my neighborhood again. "Tooommm, kitty, kitty, kitty, kitty, kitteee...." I called. As I passed my neighbor's garage, I could hear a faint meowing. Joy! Elation! And then, overwhelming dread. THAT garage. My neighbors were known to be members of the Ku Klux Klan (and probably Hoarders Anonymous, the antique farm equipment edition). The floor of that garage hadn't been seen in years. My brother Steve said that Jimmy Hoffa was hidden there, too. I was friends with the youngest member of that family, Jeremy, and our plans to host a haunted house in that garage had been thwarted the last few years. I wonder why...

But being friends with Jeremy had its benefits. I knew how to pry the lock open on the garage and get in through the door. I peered in through the mass of farm equipment, all of those sharp, rusty, edges, and at the very scariest corner (you know, the one with all the spiders), there was my fur baby. Tom had been beaten up very, very badly. He was covered in scrapes and more than a few deep gouges were taken out of his fur. He was all curled up in a spider-covered shelving unit, licking his wounds and mewing in pain. My heart melted and so did my fear. I planned to get there the only way I knew how, by climbing gingerly over all of those jagged implements, all of those tarps covering unknown crevices and flesh-impaling pieces, and made my way to my cat. My kitty. I scooped him up in my arms and made my way back the same way I came in, proud of myself for finding him, and proud of vanquishing my fear of that garage. I got him home, and coldly informed my stunned mom that he was going to be okay. Tom had the last laugh here, though. Not too long after, that grey cat got a name. Tom got into a knock-down, drag-out, tufts-of-fur flying fight the likes of which the intersection of North Park and Henrietta had never seen. Tom ripped the ear off of his enemy, and that cat never bothered him again.

From that point on, we knew that cat as Van Gogh. Evil, I know, but my cat had conquered his territory and was now the king.

Monarchs don't live forever, though it seem like Tom did. He survived until 1998, the year after my mom passed away. He was twenty-one years old.

I went crying to my brother's house after he died. My brother Joe admired Tom, called him the toughest cat he ever knew. "He was a great cat, wasn't he?" I said, sobbing.

"No," my brother said, gently. "He was the best."

ELLA

Ella, the second official member of the United Furry Front, came into my life in 1999. It was after the loss of my mom and Tom, that king of all cats, that made me long for another kitty companion. Cats were a better fit for me than dogs at the time, because of my journalism job and my terrible work hours (most of which, of course, was unpaid overtime). The funny thing with this member was, I was determined at first to find another black and white cat. I missed Tom so much! So, off I went to the Macomb County Animal Shelter. It was there that I saw firsthand why it would suck to work at a place like that. The shelter had a room chock full of unwanted cats, all sharing a few meager bowls of communal food and about two litter boxes. I was allowed to pick a few cats and share a few minutes with each to bond with them. I was looking, of course, for the tuxedo kitties so I could "find another Tom." I was peering around, not very excited about the cats there, because most of them were crouching in fear or just plain not excited to be looked at. I felt some rubbing at my legs. I looked down, and there was the fluffiest kitty I had seen in a long time. She cooed, purred and rubbed against my legs again. A calico kitty with various shades of brown and black in her fur. Yep. I was a goner. Minutes later, I was out the door with Ella (her name was Lucy on the papers, but I changed it officially to Ella Mayfield, named after both Ella Fitzgerald and Curtis Mayfield).

Ella strutted around my house for the next fourteen years with such an attitude. She always had a long silky coat and a very short temper with other cats. But the personality always shone through. In her first few years with me, she was the ultimate lap cat, coming to my bed every night and then, waking me up at two o'clock on the dot, every morning, to lick my face.

Her antics were hilarious because she did not hold back her emotions.

She perfected the resting "bitch" face that so perpetuates memes today. She'd look like she was angry, when in fact, she was really not.

She was a little hoarder kitty that kept stuff by her side, even when she slept, and if you took it, there was hell to pay. She'd glare at you, growl, hiss and spit. With me, however, she was the most loving cat.

In later years, I ended up relying on her as my most elder member of the United Furry Front.

I had a roommate when I first got Ella. Mark was his name, and he had adopted a miniature greyhound he named Max. Max and Ella didn't really get along so much—they more or less likely put up with each other. But every once in a while, they tag-teamed on some diabolical quest. Mark and I had eaten at this awesome place in Corktown, where I had a sublime pork loin. I complimented the chef on the meat, and he was so pleased he gave me a choice cut to take home with me. I got home and placed it on a high table where Max (and Ella, I assumed) could not reach it. I went into the kitchen and came back moments later to see the takeout carton on the ground and Max and Ella licking their chops. No doubt, they enjoyed the pork loin as much as I did. Ella had leapt to the table and knocked down the carton so both she and Max could eat like the royalty they assumed themselves to be.

Ella's attitude put her on many people's radars. When Nick, my husband, came to live with me, he teased Ella to no end. We'd be sitting on the couch, and Ella would be sleeping behind our heads. All of a sudden, I'd hear a growl from Ella. Nick would act as if he didn't just goose the sleeping kitty, and I'd glare at him (and inevitably smile at the same time).

Ella's vocal personality led to many funny moments. One time, I came home and Nick said, "Look what I taught Ella to do today!" Ella was sitting on a chair next to him. Nick cranked up some heavy metal tune and then, during beats in the song, would reach down and touch Ella, which made her yowl in protest. It was hilarious, because her yowling sounded like it belonged in the song the entire time.

Ella earned the Dick Cheney nickname when my mother-in-law, Roberta, came to live with us and brought her adorable corgi, Mena. Ella would take Mena's toys away from her, and the other cats wouldn't do a thing to stop her. Neither would Mena, even though that dog was clearly bigger and stronger than Ella. One time, Roberta was playing fetch with Mena with this toy that consisted of a huge rubber ball attached to a thick rope. Ella sauntered in the room, and sat watching Mena grab the rope with her teeth and haul it back for Roberta to throw. When Roberta threw the toy, Ella laid down on it when it landed and refused to move. She cast a huge stinkeye toward Mena and started to growl. Roberta and I looked at each other in shock. Nick started laughing like hell.

"Get the ball, Mena! Get the ball!" Mena would rush over toward Ella, then stop short as the cat would growl and hiss, her paws clamped over the toy possessively.

Such an attitude. Such a kitty. My Ella.

Ella was put to sleep on October 5, 2013 after a long illness. I still miss her terribly. She was a sweet, soft, cat that will always hold a place in my soul.

TIGGER

Tigger started out life as an abandoned kitten who was nurtured initially by Feline Friends, a nonprofit cat rescue group. We adopted him from the local Petco store and brought him home at six months old in June of 2000.

At that time in my life, I was working two jobs to make ends meet and I had two quirky roommates who are friends with me to this day: Mark and Peter. Mark hailed from Ohio, but Peter came from England to try to start a new life here. Peter loved both cats; nicknaming Ella "Ellawicious" and then Tigger "Tiggeriffic." Tigger took a shine to Peter, and played with him endlessly. Tigger also had a bit of a digestive problem when he first came to our house, mainly because his previous owner had fed him people food. Within the first weeks of his arrival here, Tigger had acquired a reputation for stinking up the house with his methane emissions, all of which were SBD - Silent but Deadly. Anyway, I thought it was fitting that Peter bonded with Tigger, because our British mate had a habit of passing voluminous amounts of gas as well. So, with Tigger, he could totally relate. One afternoon, when I came home, Peter was holding Tigger on his lap and said to me, very matter of factly, "This cat is Johnny Farty Pants," in his thick English accent. Tigger then leaped off of Peter's lap, dropping another bomb on him. "Oh, you can taste it!" Peter shouted.

And, because I have a third-grade sense of humor, I thought it was hysterical. Another morning, Peter came down from his room with a sneer on his face. "What's wrong, mate?" I said. (It seems I had become English as well since having Peter move in with us.)

"Tiggah jumped up on me bed, right? And then, I heard this 'poof' and then I was surrounded by this green cloud, this, this ah, God, malingering miasma of methane!"

Mark and I were holding our sides from laughing so hard.

Tigger and Ella did NOT get along at first. Ella would growl and hiss profusely if Tigger entered the same room. All three of us humans were worried that they would never be friends. Then, the strangest thing happened: Ella and Tigger were caught upstairs canoodling.

The two cats were then inseparable, and played for hours, nonstop.

Then Ella would get in one of her moods, and start hoarding stuff again, and the hissing and spitting would commence again.

Tigger, a white cat with butterscotch patches, grew quite big after his neutering, and so Peter said he would now start calling him "Johnny Fat Pants."

Tigger loved on everyone. Shortly after my buddies Cate Caldwell and Matt Pearson got married, they'd come over and meet Nick and I for double dates. Tigger would jump on Matt's lap and get loved and leave a huge coat of white fur over his black clothes. Roberta nicknamed him "Sumo" because he was so big but so sweet.

Tigger missed Ella when she passed. He meowed at night for a long time, and rubbed endlessly at her sleeping spots.

Tigger passed away on July 27, 2014, about a week after having a tumor removed. His ashes are next to Ella's on the shelf above my bed. Both of their urns are next to Nick's ashes.

MAGGIE

Maggie, our marmalade colored tabby, is the lone survivor of the original United Furry Front, and she now shares the house with Maybelle, an adorable two-month old kitten we adopted as a stray.

Maggie herself was a found kitten back in 2001. Nick spotted her in some bushes in Louisiana, and brought her home immediately.

She's been through a lot, but she still looks quite young for her age.

She's gotten lost at least a few times, and even braved a trip as an accidental stowaway when Nick moved from Louisiana to Michigan. She had hopped into a box when they were moving, and the movers loaded her up into the truck. Nick thought she was lost forever, but thankfully found her when he and Roberta made a pit stop during the long journey. She moved in with us when Nick moved in with me.

She has an awesome personality, and is a very funny and unique cat.

She will come into the room when I come home from work, and will flop herself down on the floor, demanding that her belly gets rubbed. She, along with Ella and Tigger, stayed very close to me when Nick died of a heart attack on November 20. 2010. I could go on and on here, but I will keep it short and say that I was losing my mind and my sanity through grief, and I thought I would never recover. Since Maggie was found by Nick, I worried about her as well. She became very, very close to me and has come more out of her shell. She is now the queen of the household, and bats Maybelle back into shape when she acts out of line.

I honestly don't know what I would do without my cats.

But I know as long as I have a cat, there will always be a United Furry Front.

57.
The White Cat
John Aylesworth

The neighborhood feeds him chicken,
scraps of beef, salmon baked for dinner
left by an eight- year-old who didn't get dessert.
He skips across yards teasing terriers
and rescue dogs who walk with their owners,
caught by stop lines when they lunge to chase.
In winter, he matches the moisture
and follows the plow over side streets
scraped but covered with a thin coat
so cars can leave tracks to map where they came from
and he leaves paw prints wherever he goes
since he's the spirit of the neighborhood,
hoping for Spring and another year of green.

58.
Those Round Eyes
Whitney Stout

Those round eyes. As I scrolled down my Facebook newsfeed, it was those round eyes that initially got my attention. Being the animal lover that I am, my Facebook is crowded with animal stories; from tales of happy adoptions, to stories of abuse and how to eat vegan. Animal suffering is always something that my heart has a special soft spot for. But those eyes. Those round eyes. They told a story. His face stopped my scrolling in an instant. As I looked over the picture from the local no-kill shelter that I volunteer with, his story broke my heart. His front left leg was completely backwards. It was bent at a ninety degree angle and hanging there lifelessly. I then got "the feeling."

Throughout my life, I have experienced "the feeling." It's this sensation that arises in me when I know I am chosen. This kitten was speaking to me through my computer screen (begin the crazy cat lady comments). I have adopted many animals in my past but only a few have given me that feeling. I can't control it nor do I know when it's going to hit. Those round eyes awoke something in my soul that day. So I contacted the shelter to see what I could do to help. They informed me that he was in desperate need of a foster home. I came to find out that earlier that day, his broken leg was amputated. He was currently at a vet an hour away from my home. The wheels in my head began to turn as I tried to rationally figure out how I could help this round eyed boy. I live with my boyfriend and we already had a newly adopted kitten as well as a dog. He knows my heart and the love I have for every furry being on the planet. He also said no more pets.

He is allergic to cats and was already suffering with allergies from our one cat. So I suggested that we foster the one legged kitten. How could he say no to simply fostering this kitten and then helping him find a forever home? We would rehabilitate him, give him a safe home and then help him on his merry way. Simple, right?

So by the grace of God, my boyfriend said we could foster him. I immediately send in my foster application, get approved and get the go ahead to retrieve him from the vet. On the long drive to the vet, I relay the message to myself that we cannot keep this cat. *We are simply his foster parents and a stepping stone in his life.* Little did I know, that would be easier said than done.

I learned from the vet that his leg was broken in four places. He was a stray and no one knows how he sustained such an injury. He was walking on his broken leg for a month before he was rescued. His muscles and tendons began to grow around the injury. His four inch scar and fifteen stitches told of the horror he had endured.

On the drive home, I couldn't stop looking at him. He is staring into my soul with those big round eyes and meowing at me. He responds when I pet him and begins to purr. *Don't get attached,* I immediately remind myself. His name is Otis. The name suits him so well. He adapts well to the guest bedroom I have set up for him and actually begins to play. It's hard to remember that he is still a kitten, just with one less leg. What captivated me was his will to survive. He had no family, no love, no hope. He could've curled up in that cat carrier and given up. His love for life and ability to adapt to this hand he was dealt was absolutely amazing to me. I found myself just starting at him sometimes; fascinated by his ability to teach himself how to maneuver on three legs. He mastered jumping and running and eventually sprinted past me on the stairs (both going up and down)! He has made his way into my heart the way no other animal has. Rehabilitating an animal with such a life-changing injury was such a reward.

The real gift was given to me by my loving (and tolerant) boyfriend. On Sweetest Day, he told me I could keep Otis. I was over the moon. Watching this soul that the world tried to forget, blossom and thrive, was a precious gift given to me. This little creature reminded me that we can't control what happens in our lives. We can control however, our reaction to those in need; whether they have four legs, two legs... or three.

59.
Tiny Cat
Michelle M. Monagin

I didn't like the trip up there. Not even a little bit.

Well, maybe the car ride—I like cars. I could stand with my back paws on the seat and my front paws on the window, looking out at everything that went past. And when we got to the big thing we had to ride in my person carried me, stroking my back and scratching my ears. I always like being stroked. It sometimes seems like I can never get enough stroking since I didn't have any when I was just little. Back then, I lived in a house with about a hundred other cats and just one person. One person we all had to share. I never got any attention back then.

When I finally got my own person I was already as grown as I was going to be, though I was still smaller than any of the other cats in that place or in the other place, where they took us to wait for our new people to come and get us. And my person was good, mostly. Really nice. She played with me some every day, and she would sit and stroke my back and scratch behind my ears, and sometimes rub my stomach, for hours sometimes if I'd let her.

That's what she did when we got up to the top of that really big thing. She put me in a basket with a really nice soft pillow in it, and she rubbed my stomach for a while. It made me so happy I purred at her. I didn't notice that her other hand was pulling down a net until I was caught in it. She'd strapped me down on my side so tight I couldn't move, I could barely raise my head. I couldn't see anything or anybody that was there in that space with us, I could only see my person sitting down and strapping herself into the seat next to mine. I tried to cry out in protest then, but only a little 'mew' came out.

"It's all right, Baby," she said. "It's just for a little while." She reached out and scratched my ears, which calmed me a little bit.

It seemed like a long time, though. After a little while a noise started somewhere under me. It was a bit like thunder but it went on and on, getting louder all of the time instead of dying off like real thunder does. I would have crawled under the covers and started shivering if I had been at home when a storm started. I couldn't move at all here, but I could feel myself shivering. I couldn't hear my person anymore, even though I could see her lips moving. I couldn't even hear my own voice. She had left off scratching my ears to hold on to the armrest next to her—maybe the thunderous noise made her nervous, too.

Suddenly it felt as if someone put a pillow on top of me and was pushing down. I couldn't say anything anymore—I couldn't even breath. It felt like the pillow on top of me was pushing the air from my lungs and constricting my heart. I couldn't even lift my head. The pillow beneath me felt as hard as rock now, even though it had felt very soft when my person put me there. I could do nothing more than lay there—for what seemed like hours—while the hand I couldn't see tried to push me through the basket and around me there was the loudest sound I've ever heard.

Then, just as suddenly as it had started, the hand stopped pushing me down and I could breathe again. I lay there just panting for a moment; I didn't even have the energy to call out. I wondered if it was just me, or if everyone felt that hand pushing them down into their chairs. It was a great relief not to be pushed down so hard, but now I was as exhausted as if I had run around all day with no naps.

I heard my person's voice again—the loud sound had stopped when the pushing did, I wonder if they were related? Anyway when I heard my person's voice, I opened my eyes and saw that she had undone the top part of the straps that held her down and she was stretching. I mewed in my most pitiful voice and she turned to me immediately with soothing noises. She's very good for that sort of thing. Her hand came out and I closed my eyes, expecting a scratch behind my ear, but then she did something that released the straps holding me down.

At first I was pleased, of course, because I had been tied down for what seemed like an entire day. But as I started to stand up to stretch my back I could feel my feet leaving the basket— before I had even gathered myself to jump, I was rising up toward the ceiling! I let out a loud squawk and felt my claws going out, but I was already too far away from the pillows to reach them with my claws. I was floating away.

Just when I realized that I couldn't control my movements, that I was at the mercy of something—although I didn't have any idea of what that something might be—I felt my person take me in her arms. I was so unnerved by the whole thing that I couldn't resheath my claws and I felt them catch on her clothing and her hair. I'm sure I scratched her pretty badly. She seemed to forgive me though—she just held me and rocked me like she knew what I was thinking, like she was trying to console me.

Another reason I didn't want to resheath my claws—I mean, aside from the fact that I couldn't because of the scare I'd just had—was that I didn't want to float away from my person, even if she needed to use her hands for something else and had to let go. I'd never felt anything like this. It was as if I had become lighter than a bird—lighter than a feather on a bird's wing—but I didn't have any of a bird's instincts for flying, or its wings. I didn't know how to make myself get from one place to another if I couldn't walk or jump there. What would I do if I couldn't move around myself?

My person seemed very calm, though, almost like she had expected all of the things that had been happening. I wondered, just then, could she have known? Had she taken me into this kind of a place knowing what it would be like? I didn't like to think about that. It seemed almost a betrayal. Surely my person would not have done that to me knowing how it would frighten me. Surely...

She took me over to the side, where there was a sort of round window, and we looked out. I was astounded. It had been early morning when we went into this ship-thing, and I knew it hadn't taken us hours to get to where we were now. But it was night now. It was dark, and there were stars—stars that were brighter than I'd ever seen them before. The ship seemed to turn slightly and a sort of huge ball thing moved to dominate the window.

Or rather part of the ball thing was visible in the window with black behind it. About a third of the face I could see was visible in the window. It was like a shiny, light-blue ocean with white islands. I couldn't tell what it was, at first, but my person was murmuring to me that it was the Earth and suddenly I realized that that was where we came from. I looked at my person doubtfully for a moment, wondering if she was going to stay with me or if she was going to leave me somewhere up here where I couldn't possibly get back. She just petted me absent-mindedly, looking out the window with a smile.

As we were watching out the window something whizzed by and I flinched. It didn't hit the window, but I was completely distracted from my worries. I wondered what kind of birds they had up here. I couldn't see any flying around, except the things that flew by too quickly to be identified. It would be fun to watch birds flying around up here. I supposed it was too high for squirrels—probably too high for any trees even. I wondered where the birds perched.

My person was talking steadily and calmly the whole time. In spite of my scare, I felt myself calming in response to her calm voice and the stroking she was giving my back. After a few minutes, she pointed off to the left. I looked and saw a strange thing: it was a kind of building, hanging out there. There was a round, light green section with a whole in the middle —that looked like a donut my person had let me try once. I hadn't liked it much, I remember I had sniffed at the piece she put down for me, and then walked away.

Outside the donut were thinner pieces, not circles like the center, but something like quarter-circles, arranged in matched pairs—three matched pairs, each pair a little bit farther away from the center. They seemed to be attached to the donut—or maybe to something behind the donut, I really couldn't tell.

The weird building got bigger as we watched, until finally it seemed to dwarf our ship. It was huge! It was much bigger than our house, which I had seen from the outside when my person brought me home the first time. It was really bigger than anything I had ever seen. It was so big; I didn't have anything in my experience to compare it with. And it kept getting bigger as we came closer until it seemed to tower over our rocket. I had thought the rocket was a really big thing when I'd first seen it, but this building made the rocket seem as small as a car.

Eventually, the big building seemed to swallow us and we could only see the metal walls. Shortly after that, my person started to move toward the door. We were still floating, and even though she had hold of me I kept my claws buried in her jacket. I wondered how she was managing to move herself so smoothly.

The door from the area where our ship attached into the donut was really weird. There was no handle on it, like the ones at home, just buttons off to the side. The door didn't open until after my person had touched a button that was glowing green. We went through one door, and then we had to wait for that door to close before the next door would open. And there was a strange, full sensation when both doors were closed, just before the second door opened. It was like there was too much air in there, and it was pushing at my skin from all directions.

When we went through into the donut, though, I could feel the weight come back to my body. What a relief! I still felt lighter than I was used to, but I no longer felt that I would float away if I tried to walk or jump. I could feel my claws retracting as my body relaxed. My person was stroking my back and talking to me the whole time as she walked. She sounded pleased when I started to relax.

When we reached my house, I knew it was my house because all of my things were there. There was the box where all of my toys were kept when I wasn't playing with them. There was the set of step shelves, covered with carpet, that I could use to reach the other shelves that were around near the ceiling—so I could sit up high and see everything that was going on. Those shelves were all around the room at easy leaping distances for me. There was already water in my water dish just inside the kitchen, even though there was no food yet.

Everything smelled kind of strange, sort of new, but I could see that my person had brought all the most important things. This was my home! And this was my person's home, too. I began to feel it was unlikely that my person was going to leave me here alone.

Once I took a drink, I went out into the living room to check out my perches. I gathered my weight and jumped, just as I always had, expecting to reach the first carpeted shelf easily. But once I jumped, I went much farther than I expected. I was surprised again as the first shelf and then the second shelf went past below me. It took me a moment to recover from that, and then I realized the ceiling was coming toward me very quickly. I almost didn't manage to twist myself around before I hit. Then there was nothing for me to grab hold of with my claws so I fell back down.

I did fall more slowly than I was used to, so I could twist around again to land on my feet. I landed well, but I crouched down and pushed my claws into the carpet anyway, breathing heavily for a moment. I heard a chuckle come from behind me and I looked around. My person was standing near the doorway, watching me and when I looked at her, she made encouraging noises at me. I wasn't hurt even though I'd been surprised by how high I had jumped, so I unlocked my claws from the carpet, turned around and walked over to where my person was patting the first carpeted shelf.

I mewed and rubbed against her legs to waste some time while I decided whether to try again to jump up there and how to do it. I hadn't pushed any harder than I usually did when jumping up to the first shelf. I didn't quite understand why, but my little push seemed to have a lot more power here, so I supposed that I would just have to cut down on the amount of effort I was putting into my jumps. I wasn't sure if I wanted to try jumping up there again, but she was still making her encouraging noises and patting the shelf.

I reached up and sharpened my claws on the post, just to make sure it was really there. It was. I looked up at my person doubtfully, wondering if I should just try climbing the post as I used to do when I was much younger. But doing that would put me upside down, hanging by my claws, for part of the climb. I wondered if I would be able to do it, being much bigger now—or anyway, a little bit bigger. Maybe, if I could jump farther it wouldn't take so much effort to hold myself in that position?

My person just kept patting the shelf, though, clearly expecting me to jump right up there. I sighed. I started to gather myself to jump again. Maybe if I only pushed hard enough to make it to the couch I wouldn't overshoot the shelf, which was about twice as high. I tried that, and this time I didn't overshoot the shelf so far, even though I stumbled and I had to grab the shelf with my claws so I didn't go shooting off the other side. But at least I didn't miss it, and I was very relieved at that. I'd been worried that I couldn't jump anymore—at least not with the precision I was used to—and I was wondering how I'd manage to look down on the room as I was used to.

I rubbed my forehead against my person's side as she stroked my back, making congratulating noises. She stood for a long moment, giving me a proper rub, then she stood back a little bit and I knew it was time for me to try for the next shelf. This time I didn't push too hard and I didn't stumble on the top shelf when I reached it. That was good, I hadn't lost the ability to control my jumps even if I was jumping higher than I had expected to.

I wasn't sure if I was ready to risk the wall shelves, though— they were not carpeted, and if I slid on them I could end up sliding off. I probably wouldn't hurt myself, even if I did fall off, but it was undignified. I didn't want to fall too much in front of anyone—not even my person, who loved me no matter what.

My person didn't even suggest that I should jump any more. I suppose she realized that I wouldn't do any more just yet. She just finished petting me and walked out of the door. I wasn't worried, though. Sometimes people need time alone, just like cats do. And there were lots of things for me to look into in the new house, here, without her looking over my shoulder.

One of the first things I did was to jump to the wall shelves. It was easier to experiment when no one was looking, I didn't feel so self-conscious. So I jumped up to the first wall shelf, and I did slide a bit, just like I thought I would. I did better on the second and third shelves, and by the time I reached the forth shelf I felt like an old pro. The trick was not to push off so hard—and how hard to push off was a thing I had to find out through experiment—and to expect the surface to come up very fast under me.

So it was different, jumping from shelf to shelf here, different from my old house. But it was still possible. I went all around the room, from shelf to shelf, just because I could —and to get used to it. Then I decided to go around one more time, just to make sure, since no one else was around. And it was fun.

When I grew tired of jumping along in a large circle I decided to explore the house, to see the place where I was obviously going to spend a lot of time.

Coming down from my shelves was a trick, too. Just like I flew up much more quickly than I expected, I fell down much more slowly. The first time I had done it, I had been so surprised that I didn't pay much attention. This time when I jumped from the shelves above the couch down to the couch seat I realized that it took much longer and I landed much more softly than I am used to doing. I sat on the couch, thinking about that, for a few moments. Maybe there was something I could use that for? I decided I'd have to have a good deep think about that—but not right then.

There was a hall to the side of the couch which I assumed would take me back to the bedroom and any other rooms there might be in this house. I had to find my litter box and my person's bedroom and, really, anything else there was. I've always been a rather curious cat.

There was one room on the left, just after I left the living room, that seemed to be set up as a sort of office. I know that in my old house my person used to have an office, and everything in here seemed the same. There was a desk with a computer on top and a comfortable chair in front of it. There were more of the step-shelves so I could climb and sit high up without getting in my person's way. And there was a window with a shelf for me to lay on right under it. I jumped up on that shelf under the window—I did it without any trouble now and very little effort.

We used to have good windows, at my old house, though not quite so many of them. It was three floors up, the old house was, so I could look into the tree tops and see the squirrels and the birds playing. Quite often the squirrels would try to tease me. They seemed to know that I couldn't get to them through the windows, so they'd sit on a bough outside one of my windows and chitter at me or they'd run around their tree coming very close to my window. I often wished I could go out and chase them.

The new house seemed to be at ground level—no treetops. Out this window I could see low bushes with some sort of berry on them, a sort of purple color. I looked out that window for a while, because I could see that would be the sort of bush birds would like —somewhere to perch along with something to eat. I did see some birds flying around, but they didn't come down to the bushes. I wondered about that until I realized there was a sort of netting around the area of the bushes. The net seemed to be too small for birds to squeeze through unless they were really small. Since there were no birds around the bushes, I could only assume that there were no really small birds outside, there. Too bad.

When I realized there would be no birds on that side of the house, I went back to the big window in the living room—the living room was on the other side of the house and the window was next to the couch. This seemed to be one of those French door sort of things like there used to be at my old house, the ones that let out onto the balcony where I could sometimes go to watch the birds if my person opened the door. But this one didn't go out onto a balcony or even a porch. This French door opened right on a sort of meadow—with several different colors of flowers growing there, and with a deep green grass—that sloped down to a sort of river. And there were goats out there on the meadow!

I had seen goats, before, of course, so I knew them when I saw them again. The house where I was born was near a little farm, and the farmer kept goats. One time, when I ran away from the house, I sneaked into the farm and I saw the goats very much up close. They were huge, towering above me, and I remember I was afraid they would step on me without meaning to, or maybe they would mean it, since they were so much bigger than me. Of course I was just a kitten then—it was last year. I'm ever so much bigger now.

But these goats still looked pretty big to me. I was a little nervous for a minute until I realized that they wouldn't be able to climb through the window, even if they came over here. And they looked pretty comfortable out there. The sun didn't seem really fierce, they had grass and more bushes to eat, and there was a trough for something to drink. No, the goats seemed to me unlikely to try to come into my house.

There was other wild-life out there, too. I saw squirrels running around, jumping madly from tree to tree, though the trees were set well apart. Well, I say madly, but I could probably have jumped from one tree to another, from the way I jumped to the shelves. I suspected that these squirrels had been up here for longer, and so had time to get used to it.

There were also birds. Birds of all different descriptions. There were the normal sort of little brown birds that walk around

pecking at seeds in the grass. There were the mean blue birds —
the ones my person calls Jays—that would always swoop down at
my head whenever we went outside at the old house. There were
some of the bigger birds, the ones with black feathers, who seemed
almost ready to speak when they looked at me.

But there were other birds like nothing I had ever seen
before. There was a small black bird with red shoulders that turned
its head very sharply to look at me through the window before they
flew away into the trees. There were several big, fat sort of birds
with white or grey plumage that never flew away at all, only
pecking busily at the grass in the meadow and walking around.

There were so many different kinds of birds out there that I
just sat, watching them, for the longest time. It may have been
hours. I would normally have taken a nap sometime in that period,
but the world outside was so interesting I didn't even feel sleepy. I
just sat there, watching everything going on outside the window. It
was better than my person's television shows.

It must have been at least a couple of hours before my
person came back. I looked over when the door opened and I saw
her walk in with some sort of vegetables. I thought she had been
digging around outside. I smelled the outside as I walked toward
her, and maybe a little dirt. She put the vegetables on the kitchen
table and reached down to rub my head.

"So, what do you think, Tiny Cat?" She asked me. I mewed
in response as I rubbed against her legs.

She sat down on the couch then, making a lap for me. I lay
down on her lap and closed my eyes as I felt her hands petting my
back. What did I think? I asked myself as I drifted off to sleep. I
think I've come home.

Contributing Authors

A. J. Huffman

A. J. Huffman

Where are you from?
Ormond Beach, Florida.

Describe in one or two sentences how being friends with a cat has enriched your life.
Growing up as a country girl (in rural Western Pennsylvania), we always had cats around – lots of them.   They were so loving, and yet independent.   We can learn a lot from that.

Do you have any other pets; if so, what are their breeds and names?
Two dogs: Icarus is a Chihuahua, and Bumper is a PooPom.

If you are a writer (either by trade or compulsion) what first drew you to the craft? If you're not a writer, why did you choose to write a piece for this anthology?
I started writing in grade school.   It's just something I've always done, but I did not decide on it as a career until I was in college.   It was the only thing I could see myself doing for the rest of my life.

Alexandra Heep

Alexandra Heep

Where are you from?

I was born and raised in Germany. I moved to the USA at age eighteen in 1986. I have lived in Michigan and Virginia, before settling in Chicago, Illinois.

Describe in one or two sentences how being friends with a cat has enriched your life.

I have always loved cats, but was not allowed to have them as a child. Since then, I have had many, perhaps to make up for lost time. They were all special, but my current cat, Princess Gracie, has also saved me from giving up when stricken with ongoing debilitating health issues. That just shows that cats can be way more loyal than people.

Do you have any other pets; if so, what are their breeds and names?

We are a blended pet household that now includes one Dachshund (Wiener dog) named Adrian.

If you are a writer (either by trade or compulsion) what first drew you to the craft? If you're not a writer, why did you choose to write a piece for this anthology?

First I became a writer out of passion and to see if I could compete with native-English writers, then the craft turned into necessity when I was laid off and became ill. It was the option for survival.

Allen Kopp

Allen Kopp

Where are you from?
Saint Louis, Missouri, USA

Describe in one or two sentences how being friends with a cat has enriched your life.
People let you down. There's no better companion than a cat, and they make really good bed partners on a cold winter night.

Do you have any other pets; if so, what are their breeds and names?
Two much-loved cats: Tuffy, a Balinese, and Cody, a Siamese.

If you are a writer (either by trade or compulsion) what first drew you to the craft? If you're not a writer, why did you choose to write a piece for this anthology?
From the time I was in third grade and read "The Boxcar Children," I knew I wanted to be a writer and was never interested in being anything else. I think I was born with it, like nearsightedness.

Andrea Dietrich

Andrea Dietrich

Where are you from?

Muscatine, Iowa is my hometown, but I have spent most of my adult life now in Pleasant Grove, Utah, in the county known as Happy Valley, Utah.

Describe in one or two sentences how being friends with a cat has enriched your life.

It just makes me happy to have a cat nearby, especially when I can pet their soft fur and hear that precious purr. I think they are soothing to the soul. A house is not a home without a cat!

Do you have any other pets; if so, what are their breeds and names?

My Eskimo dog I once had was a great joy. We now have an Australian Shepherd puppy, but nothing can replace my cats: especially Callie, who died at 18 from cancer and my current black female, Razzmatazz.

If you are a writer (either by trade or compulsion) what first drew you to the craft? If you're not a writer, why did you choose to write a piece for this anthology?

I always loved writing and reading, but in 2000, I started to write poetry. Now I derive much pleasure from writing for competitions and being inspired by my poetry groups and the challenges they assign us.

Beverly Offen

Beverly Offen

Where are you from?
I grew up on a small farm in a small town outside of Chicago. I've lived in Cambridge, Honolulu, and Phoenix. But I've always returned to my home in the Midwest.

When and why did you begin writing?
I was always writing—bad poetry when I was young, good academic essays in college, creative newsletters for the college where I worked and for organizations to which I belonged. But it wasn't until five years ago, during a time when I had been reading Anne Fadiman and Joseph Epstein, that I made the belated discovery of creative nonfiction and the writing home I had been seeking.

What would you say is your most interesting writing quirk?
My writing has always had a lyrical bent, and I'm prone to slipping poetic phrases into the most straightforward of prose.

What do you like to do when you're not writing?
I read, of course.

As a child, what did you want to do when you grew up?
First, I wanted to be a cowboy and ride the range. Then I aspired to become the shortstop for the Chicago Cubs. Finally, I decided I would be a starving poet in a Paris garret.

Carol Hanson

Carol Hanson

Where are you from?
Rochester, Michigan.

Describe in one or two sentences how being friends with a cat has enriched your life.
Back in the day my mom took in a stray cat. A couple days later she asked if I would take her to the Humane Society to drop off the cat. The next day she called and asked if we could go back and pick the cat up again! Not only did she return home with Buffy, but got a feline friend for Buffy named Smokey!!! She had those cats forever! I love telling this story!

Do you have any other pets; if so, what are their breeds and names?
I have a miniature Schnauzer named Schatzi and a school of fish!

If you are a writer (either by trade or compulsion) what first drew you to the craft? If you're not a writer, why did you choose to write a piece for this anthology?
I love the creative opportunity that writing gives me.

Cate Caldwell

Cate Caldwell

Where are you from?
Detroit, Michigan.

Describe in one or two sentences how being friends with a cat has enriched your life.
I've been seeing a lot lately about the healing power of cat purrs. Whenever I am feeling unhappy for any reason, if I even look at my cats I feel better.

Do you have any other pets; if so, what are their breeds and names?
Just the four mentioned in the story.   This is creative non-fiction!

If you are a writer (either by trade or compulsion) what first drew you to the craft? If you're not a writer, why did you choose to write a piece for this anthology?
I've been writing ever since I can remember.   I've always enjoyed telling stories.

Connie Marcum Wong

Connie Marcum Wong

Where are you from?
I was born in Kansas but after three and a half, I grew up in Los Angeles and for the past thirty-five years, I have lived in Hawaii, on the island of Oahu.

Describe in one or two sentences how being friends with a cat has enriched your life.
My cat Tommy, named that because he is a Tom Cat, has been a joy in my life. He is affectionate and loves to lay in my lap and purr. He has to inspect anything and anyone who enters our home. The most wonderful thing he does for me is make me laugh.

Do you have any other pets; if so, what are their breeds and names?
No.

If you are a writer (either by trade or compulsion) what first drew you to the craft? If you're not a writer, why did you choose to write a piece for this anthology?
I have been seriously writing poetry for the past fifteen years. I love to read, and poetry captures all my senses and is what I enjoy most. Poet Lord George Gordon Byron inspired me to begin writing.

Connie Marcum Wong has been the Web Mistress of a private poetry forum *Poetry for Thought* since October 1999. Her poetry has been in many publications, anthologies, magazines, and e-zines over the years.

She published her first poetry chapbook, *Island Creations* in 2005. In 2007, *Heart Blossoms* was published. In January 2010, an anthology of Poetry for Thought members poetry entitled *A Poetry Bridge to All Nations*, was published by Lulu Enterprises, Inc. Connie created the 'Constanza' poetry form in 2007 and the Con-Verse form in 2010. Connie has three grown daughters and one son and has lived with her husband in Hawaii since 1980.

Daniel P. Barbare

Daniel P. Barbare

Where are you from?
Greenville, South Carolina.

Describe in one or two sentences how being friends with a cat has enriched your life.
Ashley was the most sweetest cat.   I had to give her up when we moved, but she always gave me company.

Do you have any other pets; if so, what are their breeds and names?
Miley is our part Labrador part hound.   She was found in the country.

If you are a writer (either by trade or compulsion) what first drew you to the craft? If you're not a writer, why did you choose to write a piece for this anthology?
It is sort of a therapy for me.   I just felt like I had material and something to say about the subject.   And I adore cats.

Danny P. Barbare has been published locally, nationally, and abroad. His poetry has appeared in *Doxa, Blood and Thunder, Dewpoint, Assisi Online Journal, The Santa Clara Review, The Round, Watershed*, and many other online and print journals. He works at a local YMCA in Simpsonville, SC. and has been writing poetry for thirty-three years. He has several books available at amazon.com: *Love Poems and Gathered Poems*.

David H. Kelton

David H. Kelton

Where are you from?
Michigan.

Describe in one or two sentences how being friends with a cat has enriched your life.
Every cat I have had has been a great friend.   Animals seem to have a way of knowing when you need comfort and are able to provide it in a way humans, with all their sophisticated communication, cannot.   Cyrano's ability to deal with human things like doors and faucets and files and faucets really drove home just how intelligent animals can be.

Do you have any other pets; if so, what are their breeds and names?
Our current pets are the cats Maya and Miguel, and the Rottweilers Sophie and Cooper.   Before them, our cats were Cyrano and Spooky and the Rotweilers Roxy and Mojo.

If you are a writer (either by trade or compulsion) what first drew you to the craft? If you're not a writer, why did you choose to write a piece for this anthology?
I had been interested in writing for some time, but it was Charlotte Fullerton (a cartoon screenwriter) who convinced me that if I like writing I really should pursue it.

Deborah Guzzi

Deborah Guzzi

Where are you from?
I was born in Maine.

Describe in one or two sentences how being friends with a cat has enriched your life.
I have always had cats, they teach independence. Cats are affectionate and smart.

Do you have any other pets; if so, what are their breeds and names?
No.

If you are a writer (either by trade or compulsion) what first drew you to the craft? If you're not a writer, why did you choose to write a piece for this anthology?
The trials of life drew me to writing, it aids in emotional cleansing, healing and growing.

Diane Gooding

Diane Gooding

Where are you from?
Conyngham, Pennsylvania.

Describe in one or two sentences how being friends with a cat has enriched your life.
Being friends with a cat has enriched my life because they provide unconditional love, entertain us with their humor, and teach us some very valuable lessons.

Do you have any other pets; if so, what are their breeds and names?
My husband I have cats, Max & Frosty, Sarah the parakeet, and five Zebra Finches.

If you are a writer (either by trade or compulsion) what first drew you to the craft? If you're not a writer, why did you choose to write a piece for this anthology?
Writing is a form of therapy for me. I have been sharing my writing with my friends and one of those friends told me about *Write to Meow.*

Elisabeth Ward

Where are you from?
I now live in rural southern California, but I lived in New York State for forty years as an adult, and grew up in the Midwest.

Describe in one or two sentences how being friends with a cat has enriched your life.
Cats bring out the rhythmic and tactile side of life. Why would we want to live without that —or without them?

Do you have any other pets; if so, what are their breeds and names?
We have a Weimaraner and an English pointer, three Icelandic horses, a small herd of cashmere goats, and a smaller flock of chickens. All of them love, and are also enriched by, cats.

If you are a writer (either by trade or compulsion) what first drew you to the craft? If you're not a writer, why did you choose to write a piece for this anthology?
I am a writer (www.elisabethward.com) and need to write for the same reason I need animals: the opening of other worlds to better understand ours. We need this understanding to eliminate the need for euthanasia and animal cruelty in general. You do a great job there.

Gabrielle Gamache-Nettles

Gabrielle Gamache-Nettles

Where are you from?
I am from Michigan, born and raised here... Lived my entire life on the edge in Eastpointe.

Describe in one or two sentences how being friends with a cat has enriched your life.
My cats have made me who I am today. I pretty much love all animals, but cats and I have a deep, abiding bond. I get them, and they get me.

Do you have any other pets; if so, what are their breeds and names?
My home is blessed with two dogs; a cardigan corgi named Mena, and an Australian shepherd named Silvio.

If you are a writer (either by trade or compulsion) what first drew you to the craft? If you're not a writer, why did you choose to write a piece for this anthology?
I was a journalist for twelve years before I decided to stop the crazy unpaid overtime hours and turned to the postal profession. I went into screenplay writing because my imagination suits it rather well.

Why did you choose to write a piece for this anthology?
I had just lost two cats, and my stories about my furbabies needed to be out there, in one form or another.

Gay Pawlak

Gay Pawlak

Where are you from?
South Lyon, Michigan.

Describe in one or two sentences how being friends with a cat has enriched your life.
Every time I look at a kitty cat I have a smile on my face, they make me happy and can make anyone happy if humans would open their homes and hearts to them.   Even feral cats, just watching them play and stalk brings joy.   They are true hunters and survivors.

Do you have any other pets; if so, what are their breeds and names?
Coco and Mimi; Shih Tzus.

If you are a writer (either by trade or compulsion) what first drew you to the craft? If you're not a writer, why did you choose to write a piece for this anthology?
To help Grey Wolfe in assisting with helping animals.

G.C. Smith

G.C. Smith

Where are you from?
Beaufort, South Carolina; Lady's Island.

Describe in one or two sentences how being friends with a cat has enriched your life.
Furball cats are both diabolical and loveable, both traits enrich life.

Do you have any other pets; if so, what are their breeds and names?
No.

If you are a writer (either by trade or compulsion) what first drew you to the craft? If you're not a writer, why did you choose to write a piece for this anthology?
I wrote professionally as an economist, for a hobby, I have four novels and a book of poetry.

GC Smith writes novels, short stories, flash fiction, poetry. Sometimes he plays with dialect, either Cajun or Gullah-Geechee ways of speaking. Smith's work is published in many periodicals. He has four novels, *White Lightning—Murder In The World Of Stock Car Racing, THE CARBON STEEL CARESS, A Johnny Donal Lowcountry P.I. Novel, In Good Faith, A Johnny Donal P.I.Novel* and *MUDBUG TALES, A Novel In Flashes, Wit' Recipes*. Smith also has a poetry book, *A Southern Boy's Meanderings*.

Jen Camilleri

Jen Camilleri

Where are you from?
I am from Highland, Michigan.

Describe in one or two sentences how being friends with a cat has enriched your life.
The best thing about being friends with a cat is that you can tell them all your problems, cry out all your tears, and confess all your secrets. Their response is usually an eye roll followed by a haughty stare As they remind me to get over myself and move on, and while I'm up, I should make them some dinner.

Do you have any other pets; if so, what are their breeds and names?
I have a dog Edison who is a five year old Terrier mix. I also have four cats, Finnigan, Foster, Sophie and Truman. Edison is a rescue dog from Almost Home and the four cats were strays/feral/abandoned that found their way into my heart and home.

If you are a writer (either by trade or compulsion) what first drew you to the craft? If you're not a writer, why did you choose to write a piece for this anthology?
Writing is my way of relaxing and getting my thoughts down on paper. It also helps me avoid household duties such as laundry and dishes.

John Aylesworth

John Aylesworth

Where are you from?
Athens, Ohio.

Describe in one or two sentences how being friends with a cat has enriched your life.
We had a cat named Lucy for seventeen years that always purred when I picked her up and even though I've been around cats all of my life, she will probably be my favorite. I will always love her.

Do you have any other pets; if so, what are their breeds and names?
Wally, a golden doodle, and Sophie, a mixed breed rescue dog that we found in a shoebox along Peach Ridge Road.

If you are a writer (either by trade or compulsion) what first drew you to the craft? If you're not a writer, why did you choose to write a piece for this anthology?
When I was in junior high school, I started a story that was an assignment and it took over. It seemed to be writing itself. When I write, I hope for that feeling.

John Bayley

John Bayley

Where are you from?
White Lake, Michigan.

Describe in one or two sentences how being friends with a cat has enriched your life.
We've had cats in our house for more than twenty years. Each has had a memorable and unique personality, and all have brought us great joy.

Do you have any other pets; if so, what are their breeds and names?
Three dogs; Toby-Cairn Terrier, Albert - Black Lab, and Morgan-Yorkshire Terrier

If you are a writer (either by trade or compulsion) what first drew you to the craft? If you're not a writer, why did you choose to write a piece for this anthology?
I've been writing for twenty years and saw this as an opportunity to create some unique and entertaining characters.

John Mannone

John Mannone

Where are you from?
I'm first generation Sicilian born outside Sicily. Born as a U.S. Citizen in Montevideo, Uruguay, finished by toddlerhood in Buenos Aires, Argentina, grew up in Baltimore, Maryland, and been Tennessean for the last thirty-four years.

Describe in one or two sentences how being friends with a cat has enriched your life.
When I was a graduate student in physics, the professors were never around that first summer I was studying for the doctoral exams; I could only get answers I needed from my two cats, affectionately named Landau and Lifshitz, which were also the names of two celebrated theoretical physicists. The cats often had the right answers—I could see it in their eyes.

Do you have any other pets; if so, what are their breeds and names?
I love big dogs. I haven't replaced him yet, but Max, my one hundred pound Border Collie had died March 2010. I just got over my grieving.

If you are a writer (either by trade or compulsion) what first drew you to the craft? If you're not a writer, why did you choose to write a piece for this anthology?
Professionally I am a consulting scientist/engineer and professor of physics. In May 2004, my right-brain came out of comatose; I've been creative ever since. I had already written this piece because it was fun to write (I write so much serious stuff). I admire the mission of the publishers. For these reasons I submitted the work.

Mark Hudson

Mark Hudson

Where are you from?
Evanston, Illinois.

Describe in one or two sentences how being friends with a cat has enriched your life.
I had a girlfriend once who had three cats. She said, "If you won't love my cats, you can't love me." So I learned to love the cats.

Do you have any other pets; if so, what are their breeds and names?
I have a Guinea pig named Willow. I've had him for five years, he's awesome.

If you are a writer (either by trade or compulsion) what first drew you to the craft? If you're not a writer, why did you choose to write a piece for this anthology?
I've been writing and drawing since I was little. I hope to keep it going as long as possible.

Mary Ann Back

Mary Ann Back

Where are you from?
Mason, Ohio.

Describe in one or two sentences how being friends with a cat has enriched your life.
Although I don't own cats, I have a friend who does. When I visit they love to cuddle and wrap themselves around my legs. One of her kittens, Gray, purrs and jumps on me and kneads. They are soft and warm with personalities all their own. They will love you when it seems like no one else does. The real question is: how do we enrich cat's lives?

Do you have any other pets; if so, what are their breeds and names?
I have a white shepherd and lab mix named Max. He is ten years old, still a puppy in every way and when the day is done he either curls up in my lap or leans into my leg and put his head on my knee. He's a cuddle puppy, who by the way, came from the dog pound when he was six weeks old. They'd found him in a gutter.

If you are a writer (either by trade or compulsion) what first drew you to the craft? If you're not a writer, why did you choose to write a piece for this anthology?
I've been writing since 8th grade. I took many years off while raising my kids and working, but I'm glad I came back to it. I never realized how much I missed it. I'm glad to have submitted my story, *Secrets* for the *Write to Meow* anthology. Animals give us so much and ask so little in return. It's my privilege to help protect and provide for animals that are still looking for their forever homes.

Matt Pearson

Matt Pearson

Where are you from?
The Detroit area.

Describe in one or two sentences how being friends with a cat has enriched your life.
My cats remind me that it's okay to be a little lazy, a lot anti-authoritarian, moderately anti-social, and discerning about the company one keeps. You always know where you stand with a cat.

Do you have any other pets; if so, what are their breeds and names?
Just four cats, all of whom have cool origin stories.

If you are a writer (either by trade or compulsion) what first drew you to the craft? If you're not a writer, why did you choose to write a piece for this anthology?
I suppose I was first drawn to writing via a wider interest in filmmaking. I quickly learned that I'm a better writer than I am a producer and just followed that to its logical conclusion.

Melissa Grunow

Melissa Grunow

Where are you from?
Ferndale, Michigan.

Describe in one or two sentences how being friends with a cat has enriched your life.
I always wanted a cat growing up, so once I actually grew up, the first pet I adopted was a cat. They make life amusing. Cats are very individualistic creatures, and it's fun to see their personalities take shape and evolve over time.

Do you have any other pets; if so, what are their breeds and names?
I have three cats named Ani, Lola, and Phantom. I also have a husky named Duke.

If you are a writer (either by trade or compulsion) what first drew you to the craft? If you're not a writer, why did you choose to write a piece for this anthology?
I was first drawn to writing at a young age. I was an avid reader as a child, preferring to read over watching television or playing with friends. My love for stories naturally evolved into telling my own stories. I've always wanted to be a writer, but it's only within the past few years that I've been writing and publishing actively and regularly.

Robert Hosner

Where are you from?
I have lived my whole life in the Detroit area.   Currently I live in Madison Heights, Michigan.

Describe in one or two sentences how being friends with a cat has enriched your life.
I have had four cats.   They have always provided relationships that consist of a combination of companionship and solitude.

Do you have any other pets; if so, what are their breeds and names?
The poem is mainly about my cat Kit.   My daughter and I like to say she is a grouch.   This is a perhaps a vast understatement.

If you are a writer (either by trade or compulsion) what first drew you to the craft? If you're not a writer, why did you choose to write a piece for this anthology?
I've been writing since I was sixteen.   I've never focused much on publishing.   This poem is something I wrote about a year ago.

Tim Tobin

Tim Tobin

Where are you from?
Voorhees, New Jersey.

Describe in one or two sentences how being friends with a cat has enriched your life.
Cats are gentle little creatures who pass through our lives as members of the family. We miss each one who stepped into forever.

Do you have any other pets; if so, what are their breeds and names?
No other pets.

If you are a writer (either by trade or compulsion) what first drew you to the craft? If you're not a writer, why did you choose to write a piece for this anthology?
I am an author of short stories. MY wife lovers cats dearly and this is her true story. Except, of course, the ending!

William Doreski

William Doreski

Where are you from?
New England. Connecticut, Massachusetts, Vermont, Maine,
Currently living in Peterborough New Hampshire.

Describe in one or two sentences how being friends with a cat has enriched your life.
I live with eight cats and find their interaction, competition, mutual affection, and even occasional sparring both enchanting and enlightening. They know more, at a primal level, than people do.

Do you have any other pets; if so, what are their breeds and names?
Not right now.

If you are a writer (either by trade or compulsion) what first drew you to the craft? If you're not a writer, why did you choose to write a piece for this anthology?
I didn't write these for the anthology—I wrote them while I was volunteering at a local cat shelter. Writing, when I first began it and even now, seems to me a necessary way of explaining the world to myself.

Almost Home Animal Rescue League is a non-profit 501(c)(3) organization dedicated to finding loving forever homes for homeless animals. Almost Home is a 100% no-kill shelter made up almost entirely of volunteers with more than 100 dogs and cats in our care at any given time.

Almost Home is a place where frightened animals need not be frightened. Where animals with special needs are not discriminated against. A place that radiates warmth and love to all animals whether they are young or old, sick or healthy, maimed or beautiful. A place to feel safe and "BE" safe. We rely solely on the generosity of animal lovers like you. Your donation could mean the difference between the life and death of an animal.

SHELTER HOURS FOR ADOPTIONS:
Monday-Friday 12:00-5:00pm
Saturday 1:30-5:00pm
Closed Sunday

LOCATION:
25503 Clara Lane
Southfield, MI 48034
248-200-2695
www.AlmostHomeAnimals.org
AlmostHome1965@gmail.com